HAUNTED BAYOU

AND OTHER CAJUN GHOST STORIES

HAUNTED BAYOU
AND OTHER CAJUN GHOST STORIES

J.J. RENEAUX

ILLUSTRATIONS BY
WENDELL E. HALL

August House Publishers, Inc.
LITTLE ROCK

Printed in the United States of America

10 9 8 7 6 5 4 3 2 1 HB
10 9 8 7 6 5 4 3 2 1 PB

ISBN 0-87483-384-1 (HB) : $18.95
ISBN 0-87483-385-X (PB) : $9.95

Executive editor: Liz Parkhurst
Project editor: Rufus Griscom
Design director: Ted Parkhurst
Cover design: Harvill-Ross Studios, Inc.
Illustrations: Wendell E. Hall

The paper used in this publication meets the minimum requirements of
the American National Standards for Information Sciences—
permanence of Paper for Printed Library Materials, ANSI Z39.48-1984.

The names and places in *Haunted Bayou* are fictional. Any
resemblance to real people and places, past or present, is coincidental.

AUGUST HOUSE, INC.   PUBLISHERS   LITTLE ROCK

To Tess Renée,
a good listener and trustworthy critic,
"Action Jackson,"
who sparks my imagination,
and Max,
my best friend and valued mentor

Contents

Acknowledgments

The author would like to thank the many friends, family, and acquaintances whose accounts inspired the writing of these tales. Special thanks to August House and all the talented staff who work to keep storytelling alive and well.

Introduction

Some people believe in ghosts; others think they are merely figments of our imagination. Only one fact is known about ghosts for certain: people all over the world have been telling stories about them since the beginning of time.

The ghost stories in this collection have been passed down from generation to generation through storytelling. They have served not only as entertainment but as teaching tools, helping tellers and listeners remember the legends, myths, and history of their people. They have also acted as warnings, cautioning against the dangers of breaking the rules and taboos of a society. Now as then, tales of ghosts provide comfort by allowing people to face their worst fears without true danger.

The Acadian people brought superstition and ghost stories with them when they began to arrive in Louisiana in the 1760s. After living for generations in what is now Nova Scotia, New Brunswick, and Ile de Prince Edward in Canada, they became the victims of war and persecution. Forced by the British victors of the French Indian War to leave their homes, the Cajuns, as they came to be known, wandered homeless throughout the world.

When at last they found a new home in colonial Louisiana, they encountered a hostile land filled with danger. Hurricanes, snakebite, and cholera were among the maladies that threatened their fragile existence. With priests far and few between, the Cajuns relied on their own faith and understanding for spiritual protection against the supernatural forces which many believed roamed the swamps, prairies, and bayous.

Perhaps because they felt isolated from formal Catholic rituals, the Cajuns' own religious beliefs intertwined with their feelings of vulnerability and fear of the unknown. The ghostlore that developed is a hauntingly beautiful and rich tapestry, woven with traditional Cajun values and characteristic humor.

In this collection I have tried to capture Cajun ghostlore in stories that combine traditional archetypes with contemporary, original tales. Using my imagination as thread, I have pieced my own true experiences to fragments of ghostlore that I've collected through the years, thus creating ten new ghost stories. I have also included three traditional Cajun ghost stories—"The Fifolet," "The Ghost of Jean Lafitte," and "The Singing Bones"—as *lagniappe*, a little something extra. These tales provide contrast and texture to my story quilt. They also offer a glimpse into the minds and imaginations of many eighteenth- and nineteenth- century Cajun people.

Today's Cajuns are neither more nor less superstitious than any other group of people. Their ghostlore continues to survive through storytelling, whether in the schoolyards, on the *galeries*, at teenage gatherings, at kitchen tables, or through books and recordings. These days, ghost tales may include a great assortment of creatures, spirits, and bogeymen and are often told for entertainment. But those who really listen to this collection of thirteen ghost stories will be reminded of the timeless connection which links us to our ancestors and to future generations: our universal quest to understand the mysterious, eternal cycle of life, death, and life again.

—J.J. Reneaux

Haunted Bayou

Some people claim that Haunted Bayou actually exists. Other folks say it is a mythical place haunted only by imagination. Whatever the case, stories of the eerie ghost pirogue *are still told by fishermen right along with tales of "the one that got away." The idea of snagging a ghost boat was easy for me to imagine after seeing many strange things reeled in on fishing lines: cottonmouth snakes, alligators, nutria rats, a Model-T fender, and once, a hipwader with a catfish flopping around inside!*

B ob "Bubba" Johnson drove down the lonesome dusty dirt road, cussing the deep ruts and bumps that rocked his new four-wheel-drive truck and rattled the expensive boat rig he towed behind him. This was not exactly the picture he had in mind when he'd heard about "the best little fishin' hole in the Sportsman's Paradise." He hadn't expected a resort down here in Cajun country, but he wasn't prepared for a jungle either. Deep thickety swamp woods surrounded him, and a network of bayous ran like veins among the trees.

It had been miles since he passed the last fish camp. He must surely be lost. Nobody would be operating a bait shack and guide service way out here. But there was nothing for Bubba to do but keep on going since his boat trailer would jackknife on him if he tried to turn her around.

Well, he thought, *this road has got to end up somewhere. I'll get directions and still get to Haunted Bayou before dark.* Haunted Bayou. Funny name, but there were plenty of strange place-names in South Louisiana. According to his buddies on the bass tournament circuit, Haunted Bayou was the best kept secret in the South. Fish wrestled from its murky waters were said to be of legendary size.

Already, he could imagine how a mounted twenty-pound largemouth bass would look hanging up at his car dealership back in Dallas. A great salesman like himself knew how to spin a great fishing story to his advantage. Those good ol' boys would swallow his sales pitch, hook, line and sinker. He could sway the local yokels from a used truck deal into a full-blown, spanking-new four-by-four complete with a customized bass boat, trailer, and oversized motor from the Fish 'n Ski boat business he owned next door. He'd even throw in a new rod and reel as a free gift.

By the time the customers figured out they couldn't make the payments, it was too late; they had already signed on the dotted line. If the customer lost his shirt, so what? Sure, Bubba had to make quite a few foreclosures, but he turned them around fast, reselling the nearly new rigs like hotcakes to the next gullible buyer. *Maybe I'm not a nice guy,* Bubba thought scornfully, *but nice guys finish last, and they sure don't wear gold Rolex wristwatches.*

He glanced at the time and cussed. It would be dark in another hour. Where in blazes was that fish camp? Just then, he rounded the bend and saw that the road dead-ended at a large unpainted wooden shack standing on cypress log pilings. Just below the tin roof, a battered metal cola sign hung haphazardly, proclaiming: HAUNTED BAYOU FISH CAMP. A wide porch ran across the front where a double screen door displayed an old bread advertisement. A hand-lettered VACANCY sign pointed to a half-dozen shabby tourist cabins perched along the bank of the bayou.

Bubba Johnson rolled up and cut the motor. This was the "best fishin' hole" in Louisiana? His pro fishing buddies must have had sunstroke if they thought this miserable swamp hole was an angler's paradise. For all he knew, it was their idea of a practical joke to send him on a wild goose chase in search of giant bass in the Louisiana bayou backwoods. He thought of heading back. But it was getting dark, so Bubba walked up the porch steps and pounded on the door.

After a few moments, an old woman came shuffling to the door. "Ah, *bon soir*," she said warmly, "I thought I heard somebody comin'. You are here to fish, yes? Mebbe rent a cabin?"

"I heard there was some good fishing in these parts," Bubba said doubtfully. "It does appear I'm stuck here for the night. How much for a cabin?"

"That'll be thirteen dollars for tonight and I'll fix you breakfast in the morning. If you want to fish," she added, tomorrow."

So, Bubba thought wryly, *that's where they make their money. The old guy probably charges an arm and a leg to guide tourist fishermen like me.* "How much for the guide?" he asked impatiently.

She shrugged and said, "He'll charge you a little something, but that Joe, I think he likes the comp'ny more than the money. You know that ol' man loves to tell a story."

The screen door banged behind him. He turned to see a long rake of a fella with a weathered face walking inside toting a big stringer of fish. "*Ça va, chère*," he called, "I brought you some nice fish for you can make some o'that *bon coubuillon*. Ah," said the old man pausing, "I see we got comp'ny."

Bubba stepped forward and shook the old man's hand. "How ya doin' old timer? Johnson's the name, Bob Johnson, but most folks call me Bubba."

The old man's dark eyes took in Bubba. "Joe Mouton, that's me," he said, "and this here's my wife, Yvette. You lost Mr. uh, Bubba, or you're lookin' to do some fishin'?"

Bubba laughed. "Well, I've been told that you've got the best little fishing hole in the state. I was fishin' over at Toledo Bend and decided I might as well come on down and try my luck." Bubba eyed the heavy stringer of catfish Joe Mouton still held. "Is this a sampler of what that bayou holds?" he asked. "Not bad, not bad at all."

Joe looked down at the stringer. "Aw, I got these fishin' off the bank. The big bass is further down the bayou. I'll be goin' out again early in the mornin'. That's the best time to fish Haunted Bayou, at sun up and again in the evenin'. You are welcome to come, *mais sure*."

Bubba rubbed his palms together greedily. "Well, now, that sounds fine, just fine." he said. "My boat is gassed up and ready to go—"

Suddenly Joe Mouton was chuckling. "Aw *non*," the old man said, shaking his head. "We can't go in that big ol' boat, *mais non!* That bayou is filled with so many snags, it gonna wreck your boat Mr. Bubba. Naw, to get them big bass, you gotta go out in a johnboat or a *pirogue* for true. We will take my johnboat and paddle—that way we can sneak up on them, yes?" Joe's laughing eyes suddenly narrowed. "There is one thing more, my friend," he said quietly. "Me, I don't fish Haunted Bayou after dark, not ever."

Bubba threw up his hands. "Like the man said, you're the boss. If my luck is puny, I might head back to Dallas anyway. Guess I better turn in now. The early bird gets his worm, and Bubba Johnson always gets his fish."

The old woman gave him a key to cabin number three. Bubba quickly settled down for the night and was soon fast asleep. He slept deeply, yet it seemed a strange sound from the bayou invaded his dreams. In the early morning when he waked, the eerie sounds of his dream still echoed in his mind: the soft splashing of a paddle being dipped and pulled through the water and a distant low moaning.

The sun was rising as the two men walked down to the bayou where Joe kept his skiff tied. A mist swirled on the water, and all was quiet as though the bayou still slept. Joe quickly made his boat ready. Bubba Johnson, being a heavy, barrel-chested man, had considerable difficulty climbing into the narrow skiff. Joe shoved off and jumped in easily. They were soon floating downstream with the current.

The two men fished all morning. Bubba had some good strikes but nothing spectacular to show for all his effort. They broke off for noon dinner back at the bait shop, and then, after a long rest in the shade, went back out again. As the afternoon shadows lengthened, the two men drifted silently further and further down Haunted Bayou. At last Bubba, always talkative and full of himself, broke the peace. Unable to resist a captive audience, he started in to boasting and bragging to the old man.

" ... 'Course, I wouldn't say I'm a millionaire yet, but business is boomin'. Now, naturally I have to be a little ... creative sometimes, if you know what I mean," he said with a wink.

Joe looked at him. "*Non*," he said, "I don't think I do, Mr. Bubba."

"It's like this, ol' timer," Bubba said slyly. "Let's say some sap wants to buy a used car; well, I can talk him into a new, bigger model and a boat and trailer from my other store. Double profit for me, see?"

The old man shook his head and laughed softly. "There must be some rich people in Dallas for true."

"Nah, half the time these guys can't afford it. I wind up repossessing a lot of merchandise. But that's profit too, don't ya see? That's where the creative part comes in. I take back a nearly new boat, clean it up and whammo! Sell it to the next customer as a new boat. There you have it, tripled profit. That's how I bought this baby," Bubba said displaying his expensive gold watch. "And did you take a look at my boat? Now, that didn't cost chicken feed ya know."

The old man shook his head but didn't say a word.

"Now, being a businessman and all, I don't see how you folks make a go of it out here. Why, with a little investment this place could be a real hit. Add a swimming pool, golf course, hey, a theme park, that's it. Yeah, play on that cute name—Haunted Bayouland. Yeah, that's real catchy. 'Course, you'd have to drain the swamp ..."

"Drain the swamp? Aw *non*, Mr. Bubba," Joe said. Me and Yvette, we love this place. This is where we belong. No, we are not rich like you in money, but we are rich for true in ways you can't see. My papa and his before him ran this camp. My son workin' offshore will take it over when I'm gone." Joe looked hard at the other man and he leaned forward. "Have you not wondered, my friend, why we call this place Haunted Bayou?"

"I dunno," Bubba said with a shrug, "I suppose you're gonna tell me it really is haunted?"

"I will tell you something," the old man said, "the bayou has always been haunted. Strange things have been goin' on at night ever since there's been folks to tell the stories. Even the Indians believed the bayou was cursed. Later on, this was pirate country. Lafitte and his gang buried treasure out here. Some say he killed a man and buried him with the chest so his spirit would stand guard over that gold and silver. They figured folks was scared of the bayou and wouldn't come lookin' for the treasure. But there were always a few daredevils who came along to stir up the curse. They didn't believe in ghosts. When they wandered into the bayou after dark, they just disappeared. The few that did make it back told tales of seein' a moss-covered *pirogue*, and in it, the ghosts of the poor missing souls, paddlin' through the mist.

"My own *grand-père* saw the ghost of Pete Hudson. Pete was a fisherman like you, and he left his buddies to go down Haunted Bayou. Oh, they tried to warn him, but he wouldn't listen. He swore he'd explore the bayou and be out by nightfall, or he would 'smell hell'. Pete Hudson never was seen again alive, but his spirit is out there all right, along with the others that disappeared.

"I wouldn't believe it myself, but I saw them for true when I was a boy. Me and Papa was out fishin' late and found we had drifted too far down the bayou and night was comin' on. Well, out of the darkness comes a *pirogue*, all covered with moss. From a distance we thought it was some other fisherman comin' in late. But when that boat come closer, we saw it was filled with ghosts! All of them misty like and glowin' like moonlight. Papa yelled for me to paddle while he rowed. But it seemed like no matter how hard we worked, we just couldn't make no headway upstream. We were just splashin' and splashin' and still goin' slow as cold molasses. That ghost boat was almost on us, but when we come around that big curve, right up from where we are fishin' now, the curse let go of us. *Padnat*, we got to paddlin' plenty fast then, I guarantee! Ah, it's horrible to see them comin' at ya, moanin' and hollerin' for help. But that curse has got them trapped forever. They can never find their way out of Haunted Bayou."

Bubba was looking with raised eyebrows at the old man. "Well, I got to hand it to you," he said with a snort, "you had me goin' there for awhile. You would've made a great salesman, ya know that?"

Suddenly, Joe's eyes widened and stared downstream. "Well, would ya look at that?"

Bubba shifted his heavy frame as best he could and turned around, half-expecting to see a ghost. Instead he saw the biggest bass he had ever seen. It was the granddaddy of all bass. The fish sliced through the dark water and hit at Bubba's lure. He felt his line go taut and then his rod was bending nearly in half with the weight of the fish. Bubba slowly reeled him in with great effort, his arms straining against the pull. The huge bass was fighting like a champion, threatening to swamp the skiff.

Breathing hard, Bubba pulled the flopping bass out of the water. "Get my net," he hollered, "I've almost got him ..."

Just then the fish gave a mighty flap of his tail and shook the lure from his mouth. He fell back into the water and disappeared with a final splash.

"I almost had him," Bubba exclaimed, "Well, he's still

out there. It ain't over yet!"

Just then, as though the giant bass had heard his challenge, it hit at a mosquito just a few feet from the johnboat and splashed Bubba in the face.

"Why, if I didn't know better," Bubba sputtered, "I'd swear that fish was teasin' me. Look, there he is again. Come on, let's get this boat downstream. He hit once, he'll hit again!"

Bubba grabbed a paddle and began pulling it through the water. All at once he became aware that Joe Mouton was sitting there motionless, looking at him quietly. "What's the matter?" Bubba demanded. "Come on, I can get him, I know I can. Let's get this skiff downstream!"

"My friend, I think you are forgettin' somethin'," Joe said, "I told you I don't fish Haunted Bayou after dark, especially this far down. It's gonna be night soon. We got to start back now."

Bubba stared at the old man. He couldn't believe his ears. "You mean to tell me I'm gonna lose that fish 'cause of some ol' ghost story?" he asked angrily. "Not on your life. I want that fish and I mean to have it. What Bubba Johnson wants, he gets."

"Mr. Bubba, this is my boat," Joe said softly. "Like I done told ya, I don't fish the bayou after dark. You know the reason why we got to be leavin' now." The old man began to paddle the skiff upstream against the slow current.

Bubba scowled but kept his thoughts to himself. *Crazy old man! If he thinks I'm gonna let that giant bass slip through my fingers, he's wrong. We'll go on to the fish camp, but I'm getting my boat and comin' back for that bass!*

The men paddled up to the Haunted Bayou Fish Camp just as darkness fell. Bubba saw it was going to be a full moon. *So much the better,* he thought, *make it easier for me to find my way back.* He knew the place all right. He had carefully marked it in his mind: the bayou curved in a wide arc to the south, and in the middle of the stream, two large snags jutted out of the water.

Bubba waited until the old man went inside. Then he started his truck and backed his boat down the ramp and into the water. When everything was ready, he started the motor and steered his big, expensive boat down the bayou.

Up at the fish camp, Joe and Yvette heard the motor whining. "You don't think Mr. Bubba is goin' back out?" she asked. "Didn't you warn him about the curse of Haunted Bayou?"

"Oh, I told him," Joe answered, "but he didn't believe me. Could be, Yvette, Mr. Bubba is somehow s'posed to go down that bayou. He'd be meetin' up with his own kind for true. Maybe somebody wants to teach him a thing or two."

Yvette looked at Joe. "You mean," she said, nodding her head toward heaven, "Him?"

Joe nodded his head. "*Mais oui,*" he said. "It would not be the first time somethin' good came out of a curse. But, just in case Mr. Bubba is a slow learner, I'll take my skiff out and tie up to them two stick-up snags at the big curve. Don't worry about me, ol' woman, I'll watch out for them ghosts for true."

Bubba had a head start on Joe. He had already reached the two stumps. Now he was forced to slow down and ease his way through the snags. *Ol' Joe was right,* he thought, *it is thick in here. Well, I'll use my trolling motor. That's better anyway, it won't scare Mr. Granddaddy Bass.* Soon Bubba had the smaller motor purring, and he put his favorite lure on his line.

Just then, he heard splashing in the distance. It was that giant bass, it had to be. He aimed his rod in the direction of the sound and made a long cast. He reeled in the line, working the lure expertly. Another splash, nearer this time. He cast out again. Still nothing. *Come on you beautiful bass,* he thought, *open up that big mouth and grab that lure!*

The splashing was coming closer and closer. Bubba cast his lure in a long arc across the curve of the bayou. Some overhanging branches blocked his view, but he knew it must have hit on target. Immediately, he felt a great tugging on the line. "There you are," he hollered, straining at his reel. But as he fought to bring the fish in, a disturbing thought occurred to him. *Funny, that splashin' was just like what I heard in my dream. Sure did sound like somebody paddlin'.*

Suddenly Bubba froze. A strange luminous glow was coming around the bend. He tried to tell himself it was just the light of some other fishermen coming in late, but he knew better. The sound of oars splashing in rhythm drifted over the water. There was something else too. Over the pounding of his own heart, he heard a dreadful low groaning. The eerie light was brighter now, he could almost see ... There it was! A glowing moss-covered *pirogue* was moving slowly upstream. Inside sat three luminous figures, pale as moonlight, paddling furiously and groaning pitifully.

Bubba became aware again of the taut line that was bending the rod he held in his trembling hands. To his horror, he realized there was no fish on the other end; his lure had snagged the *pirogue*. He was reeling in the ghosts! "YEEOOW!" he hollered, and threw the new rod and reel over the side. In a panic, he lowered the big boat motor into the water. A push of another button and the motor roared to life.

The cries of the ghosts rose into a gruesome shrieking. Nearly terrified out of his mind, Bubba slammed the throttle in and the boat lurched forward. Relief spread over him as the boat gathered speed. But suddenly the hull of the boat rammed into a partially submerged stump. Bubba was thrown to the deck and water began to gush in through the tear in the fiberglass.

The ghost boat was gaining on him now. The spirits were making a fearful racket, groaning and moaning. The ghost at the oars cried out, "HELP US! WE ARE LOST, SHOW US THE WAY OUT!" The glowing figure in the stern joined in the clamor, shrieking, "WE WANT OUT, WE WANT OUT!" while a ghostly pirate in the bow brandished a cutlass and screeched, "WAIT UP MATE, WHAT'S YOUR HURRY?"

Bubba looked around in desperation. The boat was

sinking. There was no doubt about it, he was going to have to swim for it. Where was his life preserver? Now he remembered, he didn't have one. The ghosts were rowing closer. Their burning eyes weakened him with fear, but he climbed to the edge of the swamped boat and flung himself into the cold water.

The current upstream, usually slow, now flowed against him like a wall. Bubba kicked and splashed with all his might but he made little headway. Up ahead two jagged stumps loomed before him. *If I can just get to those snags, maybe I can make it past the curve and break free*, he thought, remembering the old man's story. Bubba swam frantically, but he seemed to be moving in slow motion. At that moment, he would have traded everything he owned to wrap his arms around those cold, slimy stumps. It seemed as if his life was passing before his eyes. All those rotten deals he'd made, all those cheating lies weighed him down in the water. As he fought the current, his heart struggled against a wave of guilt and regret. As Bubba Johnson thrashed in the inky water, he bargained with heaven, hoping to make the deal of his life.

Suddenly, up the bayou he saw a light. He cringed in terror. More ghosts, he was trapped! Then he heard a voice, a human voice, call out and echo down the bayou, "Swim to the forked stumps, Mr. Bubba, and hang on! I'm comin' fast as I can!"

It was Joe Mouton in his skiff. *Good ol' Joe!* The sound of the old man's voice gave him strength. Bubba overcame his panic and swam with renewed hope for the stumps. The force of the current pushed against him, but he kept swimming until he could almost grasp the first snag. With his last bit of strength, he lifted his numb, trembling hand from the water. His hand fell on the rotting stump, and he held on to it for dear life.

The old man was paddling as fast as he could in a deadly race with the ghost *pirogue*. The stakes were high for him, but the prize—a man's life—was priceless. At last, Joe pulled alongside the snags and held out his hands. Bubba grasped Joe's hand and flopped heavily into the skiff. "Get to paddlin', Mr. Bubba," Joe ordered, "we got to get outta here, *vite-vite!*"

Bubba turned around to reach for a paddle and saw the ghost boat looming behind them. The ghosts were howling so fiercely that he froze in fear. "C'mon, Bubba, PADDLE!" the old man shouted, "they can't make it around the curve but WE CAN!" Bubba grabbed the paddle, shut his eyes tight, and went to work. He didn't open them again until he felt the skiff bump gently against the bank. He opened his eyes wide and saw they had made it to the fish camp. He peered behind him into the dark bayou. All was quiet.

The next morning Bubba stood on the bank, looking out at the twisting brown water. "Ça va, my friend," called ol' Joe. "You are lookin' good this mornin' for a man who caught a ghost boat instead of a fish. Oh, man, Yvette laughed at that she did!" Joe walked over and stood beside Bubba. "Well, Mr. Bubba, you didn't get your giant bass," he said with a twinkle in his dark eyes, "but you sure got a whale of a story, eh? I bet you not gonna sell too many big ol' boats with that tale!"

Bubba grinned at the joke, but when he answered his eyes were serious. "Joe," he said, "you saved my life last night and I'm in your debt. If there's ever anything I can do for ya'll ..."

The old man shook his head. "Mr. Bubba, you just come back and see me and Yvette, and maybe next time," he said with a sly smile, "you'll leave your big boat at home!"

Bubba laughed and looked out at the water again. "You know," he said, "when I was clinging to that stump, I could see that all those crooked deals I've been making were wrong. I made a promise to straighten everything out. Guess you must really think I'm a fool. Bragging the way I did, then getting myself in trouble on the bayou, nearly drowning and making deals with ..."

"*Le Bon Dieu?*" Joe asked with a chuckle. "My friend, I am sure He understands. After all, He was a fisherman too, eh?" The two men laughed heartily and strolled up to the fish camp for a cup of Yvette's strong coffee. Behind them, the morning sun glinted like gold on Haunted Bayou. All in all, it looked like a good day for going fishing.

The Fifolet

Here is a traditional story which describes the cause and cure of the eerie burning balls of light called feu de follet *or* fifolet—*known elsewhere as the will o' the wisp or just plain ol' swamp gas. It is said that a sighting of a* fifolet *indicates a treasure is buried nearby. Follow the floating* fifolet, *and it will lead you to hidden riches. But be wary, for the* fifolet *is a master of tricks and will do its best to lead wandering souls astray.*

Down around the great Atchafalaya swamp, there was an old man called Medeo who had mastered the evil arts. At night this wizard would go in secret to a corn shed, and once inside, he'd shimmy out of his skin like a snake, roll it up, and hide it in a shadowy corner. Then, by the power of his evil spell, the wizard would change himself into a *fifolet*, a burning, shining ball of blue and white flames. He'd float out to the swamp, dancing and bobbing through the darkness, tempting all to follow him to destruction and death.

People in the village began to disappear. Others followed the *fifolet* and fell under the wizard's spell. They became like the living dead, forced to slave for Medeo and

obey his every command.

In the village there was a young woman called Zula. She was curious as a cat. What was happening to the people? They had once laughed and danced, but now they only stared like owls and walked with shuffling feet. Zula kept her eyes and ears open. Soon she saw that old Medeo entered the corn shed as a man … but left as a *fifolet.*

She went to the people and cried, "Medeo is the *fifolet!* He is slowly killing us just as he killed those who followed him and never came back. Can't you see that Fifolet will not stop until he gets us all? We have to fight him!"

But the people had no will of their own. They hung their heads in silence; they were afraid. Zula was frightened too. She feared Fifolet would lead her own children away, never to return. Zula waited and watched until one dark night she saw Medeo enter the corn shed. Softly, softly, she crept up to the shack. Through a crack in the wall she watched as the wizard cast his spell. He shed his skin and hid it in a dark corner. Then, before her very eyes, he changed himself into a burning ball of blue and white flames and floated out of the shed.

When Fifolet was long gone, Zula ran back to her *cabane.* She sat on her *galerie,* thinking hard. *How do I fight fire?* she wondered. *How do I fight a fifolet fire?*

Suddenly Zula leaped to her feet and ran into her cabin. She filled her deep apron pockets full of the things she would need to fight, and with the help of *Le Bon Dieu,* destroy the *fifolet.*

Quietly, Zula slipped into the shed and found the

obey his every command.

In the village there was a young woman called Zula. She was curious as a cat. What was happening to the people? They had once laughed and danced, but now they only stared like owls and walked with shuffling feet. Zula kept her eyes and ears open. Soon she saw that old Medeo entered the corn shed as a man ... but left as a *fifolet.*

She went to the people and cried, "Medeo is the *fifolet!* He is slowly killing us just as he killed those who followed him and never came back. Can't you see that Fifolet will not stop until he gets us all? We have to fight him!"

But the people had no will of their own. They hung their heads in silence; they were afraid. Zula was frightened too. She feared Fifolet would lead her own children away, never to return. Zula waited and watched until one dark night she saw Medeo enter the corn shed. Softly, softly, she crept up to the shack. Through a crack in the wall she watched as the wizard cast his spell. He shed his skin and hid it in a dark corner. Then, before her very eyes, he changed himself into a burning ball of blue and white flames and floated out of the shed.

When Fifolet was long gone, Zula ran back to her *cabane.* She sat on her *galerie,* thinking hard. *How do I fight fire?* she wondered. *How do I fight a fifolet fire?*

Suddenly Zula leaped to her feet and ran into her cabin. She filled her deep apron pockets full of the things she would need to fight, and with the help of *Le Bon Dieu,* destroy the *fifolet.*

Quietly, Zula slipped into the shed and found the

wizard's skin. She shook it out until it hung from her hands like a pair of longjohns flapping from a clothesline. The skin was dry and cool to the touch, like the skin of a lizard. She dipped a hand into her apron pocket and began to scoop something out. Zula quickly filled the wizard's skin to the neck with salt and garlic and a *grand beaucoup,* a big ol' bunch of *très chaud,* hot, hot cayenne pepper!

Just then she heard a crackling, burning sound at the door. *Vite-vite,* she hid herself in the shadows. The shed was lit up by the eerie, bobbing light of the *fifolet.* Its voice mumbled strange words that Zula had never heard before.

In an instant Medeo was back in his human skin. But all of a sudden that wizard began to itch and twitch, itch and twitch, until he was jumpin' and jitterbuggin' all over the place. He howled out, "Ohhh yeyiiee! Ohhh yeyiiee! I'm burning!" The wizard saw Zula. "You did this!" he screamed. "I'm gonna getchoo!"

Medeo's beard was burning with blue-white flames, and his eyes glowed like red-hot coals. Thick smoke poured from his nose and ears, and sparks flew from his fingers. Medeo leaped to grab Zula, but as he jumped into the air, he exploded like a firecracker into a roaring fire. "Ohhhh yeyiiee!" In a flash he burned up to a crisp and all that was left of that mean old wizard was a little pile of smoking ash.

The people of the village were free of the *fifolet's* curse. Once again they laughed and danced and sang. To this day they've never been bothered again by any old *fifolet,* because now they know how to fight *fifolet* fire—with a *beaucoup* of hot-hot cayenne pepper!

Rapadeen and Marie

This tale began with a fragment of a ghost story told by a middle school student in Louisiana. Her brief tale described the tragic drowning of a young woman. I was haunted by the images her story conjured in my mind. In time, my own experiences and family stories merged with the account and a new tale rooted in tradition was created. This tale is named for the Cajun girl Rapadeen, who shared her gift of story with me.

The Atchafalaya river flows deep and swift before it spills into an unpredictable puzzle of lakes, bayous, cut-offs, and swamps known as the Atchafalaya Basin. Many tales are told of the mysteries of *Le Grand Basin* and the ghosts who wander its ever changing waters.

Drift down a lonesome bayou to the edge of the Atchafalaya swamp and you might find a long-forgotten little cabin leaning sadly among the moss-hung cypress trees and the dagger-like blades of palmetto. Thick green vines twist and twine around the rotten railing of the *galerie*. The open windows are dark, and the door hangs crazily from its rusted hinges.

Inside the dusty *cabane* an old plank table limps on

three legs, and the wooden skeletons of a pair of broken chairs lie on the floor. The walls are papered with the yellow, faded pages of an old-fashioned mail-order catalog. Here and there the paper has rotted from the walls. Light peeks in through the cracks but fears to enter the gloomy room. The only signs of life are the spiders busily spinning their lacy webs to the distant drumming croak of the *wawaron*.

The people who passed their lives here have been gone a long, long time. But on a certain night each year, the cabin comes to life. Trappers and fishermen swear they see lights and the ghostly figures of two women sitting at the table. The sound of their quiet talk and gentle laughter floats across the water, and the air is filled with the sweet fragrance of summer roses. The old ones will tell you these shades are the ghosts of Mama Marie and her daughter Rapadeen, that *jolie fille* with the long, black, flowing hair.

Many years ago, Rapadeen lived with her mama, papa, and her brother Guillaume in the little cabin. Papa braved the swamp day after day, fishing and trapping to make a living. But the Basin respects no man. Its restless wandering waters can fool even the most seasoned captain. One day, Papa went out to run his trotlines and never returned. He disappeared without a trace.

The family he left behind was soon near starvation. They all worked hard, but Guillaume was only a boy, and thin, sad Mama fell ill from the endless struggle against the merciless swamp. Their survival rested upon the young, strong shoulders of Rapadeen.

The girl roamed the swamp, trapping, fishing, and picking moss to dry and trade for the things they needed to survive. She had learned much from her papa and tried her best to keep them all fed. But the hard work was beyond her strength. She worked until her hands bled and her back ached but it was never enough. Too often, hunger was an unwelcome visitor to the little *cabane.*

These were the years of the Great Depression. Bad luck and hard times flooded the Basin. Everybody had their own burden of poverty to bear, but Rapadeen could only think of her own trouble. The girl hated her life. All around her there was only work, work, and more work. If only she could run away to New Orleans! She'd marry a handsome, rich man and live a life of ease. She'd sip her *café* from a delicate china *demi-tasse* and dress in the latest styles.

At night she dreamed over a mail-order catalog, imagining she was one of those pretty city girls in their fancy store-bought dresses. When the cabin was dark and still, she lay awake in bed wishing with all her heart that she could escape the swamp and go to New Orleans. At last, the exhausted girl drifted into a sea of dreams filled with silk dresses and fine gentlemen.

By the age of sixteen, Rapadeen was a beauty. Her eyes were dark as midnight and her skin a velvety *café au lait.* Her glossy blue-black hair rippled down her back and fell in curls to her knees. The girl was a wildflower blooming unseen and untouched deep in the swamp.

Mama Marie watched and worried over her *jolie fille.* The Basin was a dangerous place, especially for an innocent girl with a pretty face and a head full of dreams. "Beware of strangers," she warned her daughter. "Stay away from those smooth-talkin' men. To follow that kind is like chasin' a *fifolet!* They'll only trick a poor girl with promises and lead you to ruin. Soon, you will marry, *chère*, and then it will be easier for you. We are poor, yes, but we can be proud of our name. We are tied by blood to some good families down the bayou. Surely there is a young man, a hard worker, yes, who will win your wild heart," said Mama Marie, teasing her daughter.

But Rapadeen only tossed her long hair in anger. "You would marry me to any ol' mule of a man with a strong back! You think I want to stay stuck in the Basin all my life, worrying if I'm gonna have enough to eat and always wonderin' if my man is gonna come home from the swamp? You don't understand me, and you don't know nothin' about love!"

"You best put those foolish dreams outta your head, *chère*," Mama snapped. "What do you know about love? I tell you it's a whole lot more than pretty words and promises. You listen to me. Keep away from those fancy 'gentlemen' you so admire. All you got is your good name. You dirty that and no decent man is gonna have you for a wife!"

Mother and daughter argued and fought, neither of them forgetting or forgiving the anger between them. In time their deep love for one another was buried under their bitter words.

Mama Marie feared Rapadeen would fall prey to the

first good lookin' devil that passed her way. *It is high time Rapadeen met some nice boys,* she thought. *She works so hard, and after all, a girl needs a beau to court. If I know anything about a young girl's heart, she'll soon fall in love and forget all about her fancy dreams. But how to arrange it? A fais-dodo of course! I'll send the news down with the next supply boat. Saturday week, a fais-dodo dance at the Boudreaux camp, everybody come!*

But Mama was too late. Rapadeen had already fallen in love with a no-good scoundrel. The young rogue had discovered the girl as she made her way through the swamp, poling her *pirogue* with strength and grace. He was charmed by her beauty. *What a prize she would be on my arm,* he thought. "Hello!" the stranger called. "Wait a minute, would ya?" The girl eyed him with suspicion and began to move away from him quickly.

Rapadeen remembered her mother's warning, but curiosity about the handsome young stranger made her slow her pace. *What's he doin' way out here?* she wondered. *Maybe he is lost and needs help.* She watched the man approach her and admired the way the flickering sunlight shined on his tawny hair. He was unlike any man she had ever seen. His clothes were too fine to be messing around any old swamp. What bold ways he had, looking straight into her eyes until she felt her heart beating faster.

"Hello, what's your name?" he asked, pulling his skiff along side her. But the girl only shook her head and spoke in French. *Ah,* he thought, *she don't even talk good American, one of them Cajuns I bet.* Bowing low like a knight before his lady, the young man spoke a little French he'd picked up in New Orleans. "*Comment ça va, Mamselle?*"

Rapadeen laughed at the twangy way he talked. Flashing her prettiest smile, she spoke shyly. "*Ça va bien.*" What began as an innocent chance meeting soon became the girl's carefully guarded secret. Everyday they met in the shadows of their hideaway on an island deep in the swamp. The girl learned to understand a little of the man's funny English, but it was the message in his eyes that moved her heart.

Rapadeen had never been so happy. She believed her young man loved her and she adored him. He was going to take her to New Orleans. They would run away together. She was going to marry him and Mama couldn't stop her! Then he would buy her a red silk dress and they would live happily ever after in a fancy house in New Orleans. Her young man said it was so, and he would never lie.

Rapadeen had little way of knowing that her true love was a lowlife con man hiding out from the law. He did not love her, only her beauty. Yes, he would take her to New Orleans, but he had no intention of marrying the girl.

Lots of fellas will spend good money to have a few laughs with the lovely Mamselle, he thought greedily, *and in these hard times ya gotta make a buck anyway ya can. I reckon the sheriff down at Morgan City has forgotten that little misunderstanding over that poker game. I've been layin' low in this stinkin' swamp long enough. Time for me to get back to New Orleans. Yes sir, that girl is gonna be my ticket to the big time. No more nickel and dime poker for me! If she gives me any trouble, why I'll just give her the slip.*

It wasn't long before Mama noticed something different about her daughter. Rapadeen was very quiet. The girl was spending too much time out in the swamp. Marie was troubled but she told herself the girl was just excited. *Mais oui,* she thought, *Rapadeen is just on pins and needles thinkin' about the fais-dodo.* Mama tried to put her worries aside, but she could not rid herself of the strange uneasy feeling that pricked at her heart.

At last the Saturday of the *fais-dodo* arrived. Mama cooked a huge pot of chicken gumbo. There was fresh catfish to fry, red beans, rice, and sweet potato biscuits. All day she kept Guillaume and Rapadeen busy getting everything ready for the company.

Rapadeen did her chores lazily, for she had other thoughts on her mind. Tonight was the night she was running away. *Nobody will miss me at the fais-dodo. Mama will think I'm out visiting on the galerie or taking a stroll with the young people. By the time they find me gone, I'll be half-way to New Orleans. Mama will worry of course,* she thought with a pang. *Well, I don't care. I hate this swamp and I'm gettin' out of here!*

Suddenly she was startled from her daydreams. "Rapadeen!" Mama called, "What is the matter with you? Quit your dreamin' and set the table like I told you. Get back to work before I …"

"Before you what, Mama? I'm too old for you to boss

around anymore. You're the one who wants a *fais-dodo*, you do the work! You're just tryin' to marry me off, but it won't work, you're too late!"

"Whatcha talkin' about, girl? What d'ya mean, 'too late'?" Mama looked hard at her daughter. "You got some secret, *chère?* Yes, that is it, I see it in your eyes. You have gone against me. Who is he?" she demanded. "Who is the boy you are meeting in secret?"

"I don't know what you're talkin' about, Mama. But if there was a boy, it would be my business," the girl angrily shouted. "You can't tell me what to do anymore!"

Just then they heard shouts in the distance. "The cousins," Mama said, "they're here." Mother and daughter looked at each other coldly. "You mind me, *chère,*" Marie pleaded, "listen to your Mama." But Rapadeen only ran out the door to greet the company. A little smile twitched on her lips as everyone kissed and hugged, but her heart was like stone. Tonight she would leave forever. Then Mama would miss her for true.

Everybody was talking at once, catching up on news and enjoying all the good food. When the cool summer half-dark fell, the children ran around catching lightning bugs while great-uncle Amédée tuned his fiddle to cousin Leo's guitar and Ol' Man Joe pulled wheezy notes from his squeezebox accordion. Mamas shooed their tired little ones into the cry room and laid them down on quilt pallets.

The young folks, eager to dance, pushed the chairs and table against the walls. Soon the music started up and the ting-a-ling of a *'tee fer* triangle joined the musicians on a soulful waltz. The old ladies sat against the wall gossiping while the dancers swirled around them. In the cry room the fussy *bébés* drifted off to sleep to a Cajun lullaby of song, rhythm, and laughter.

The hour grew later and the *fais-dodo* was in full swing. The dancers two-stepped to the chanky-chank band, and the wooden planks of the cabin floor shook beneath their lively feet. Rapadeen danced with all the boys, but her thoughts were only on the man who was waiting for her out in the swamp.

At last, she passed unnoticed into the lean-to that served as a cook room and out the back door. For a moment she looked behind her through the open doorway and saw Mama dancing with Guillaume in the golden light. *How young and pretty Mama looks tonight,* she thought. *Maybe she will be happier when I am gone.* Tears stung the girl's eyes as she turned and ran into the night.

Rapadeen climbed into her *pirogue* and pushed off. She poled it deeper and deeper into the swamp, searching for her love's signal: a swinging lantern light. A full moon shined down, casting eerie shadows on the glittering water and turning the mossy cypress trees into hovering giants. The swamp that she knew so well by day looked different in the moonlight. Which was the right channel of water to the hideaway? She turned one way and then another only to find herself going in circles.

All around her the Basin was alive. The *wawaron* croaked for rain and the *chouette* hooted to its young. Branches rustled and water splashed as creatures slithered and darted out of her path. Mossy branches and cobwebs caught in her long flowing hair.

I must be close now, she thought. "*Cher?* Where are you?" she called softly. She listened for an answering voice but only heard the whining of mosquitoes. Just then she saw a flashing light. *It's him!* she thought. *He does not call out for fear we will be caught.* She quickly turned the *pirogue* toward the light. The girl pushed along as swiftly as she could, but the light always danced before her in the distance.

Once again she called out, "Please, wait for me. I can not go so fast."

For a moment Rapadeen lost sight of the light. Then, rounding a bend, she saw their hideaway and the swaying light beckoning her forward. Rotting snags of timber stood like jagged teeth in the swift stream, blocking her passage to the other side.

A cypress tree felled by lightning stretched from the side of the channel to the island. The girl pulled up to the cypress and tied her *pirogue* to a branch. She gingerly climbed out of her skiff onto the tree trunk. Slowly, step by step, she felt her way across the slick log bridge toward the burning, flickering light. Beneath her the restless current churned with whirlpools and eddies.

Just then a heavy cloud hid the moon's face, and the swamp was drenched in an inky darkness. Rapadeen halted, unable to see her way. "Please, *cher*, come and help me," she begged. "Open up your lantern and raise it high so I can see you." But the only reply was the wind rattling through the branches.

"Why don't you answer me? We are safe now. Talk to me—I know you are there!"

A strange whirring hummed in the black night. "Stop it, *cher*," the girl demanded. "Why do you tease me?"

The eerie whirring sound rose higher and higher until it became a shrill moan. Suddenly, Rapadeen's blood ran cold. The light was growing brighter with an unearthly blue glow. Shrieking and spitting flames, it burst into a spinning fireball. The girl's eyes were wide with terror as she stood frozen like a statue on the log bridge. The blue flaming ball was spinning crazily toward her, faster and faster. At last her terrified mind forced her lips to scream the name of the horrid thing.

"*FI—FO—LET!*" Rapadeen turned in panic to run. One step, two steps. It was almost upon her. She could feel its fiery heat on her back. Three steps, four—the girl twisted her ankle and felt herself slipping from the wet log bridge. Frantically she tried to right her balance, but it was no use. She was falling down, down, until she splashed into the cold murky water.

It seemed she was falling forever, plunging deeper and deeper into darkness. At last she touched the muddy bottom. Then she was rising, her lungs bursting for breath and her heart pounding wildly in her ears.

All at once Rapadeen was jerked downward into a whirlpool. She struggled desperately to free herself, but a lock of her flowing hair caught fast in a tangled web of roots. With the last of her strength, the girl fought against the current to save her life. The whirlpool sucked her breath away until her lungs were heavy with cold water. As she sunk deeper and deeper, Rapadeen knew all was lost; her life was slipping away.

Her hands quit their thrashing, and a strange calm came over her. An image of Guillaume and Mama waltzing in the golden light of home filled her mind. A ways off in the black distance a beautiful light was shining. She felt no fear as the glow moved towards her. Then Papa was there with her. All earthly sight and sound ceased as Rapadeen followed him into that heavenly brilliance. He lead her into eternity, and Rapadeen wandered lost no more.

Cheated of its prey, the greedy *fifolet* spun away in search of other lost, wandering souls. Even as the girl lay dying in the depths, it sensed a greedy-hearted man headed its way. A few miles off, the young rogue stopped his skiff. Holding his lantern high, he peered into the night, looking for some familiar landmark to guide him.

In the west a blue flickering light danced against the night, tempting him to follow. As the man turned his skiff towards the glow, the flame burned brighter. The *fifolet* would feast on the stranger's rotting soul that night and leave the scraps for the 'gators.

Back at the *cabane,* Marie waited anxiously for news of Rapadeen. They had been searching for the missing girl since midnight. The women were brewing another strong pot of *café noir* when Marie suddenly bolted up from her chair, her heart tolling like a death bell. "Rapadeen is dead!" she cried out, falling to her knees. "No, it cannot be!"

"Let us wait and pray" said the women, "Do not think such thoughts." But it was no good. Marie heard her daughter's cries deep within her own soul and felt the chill of death enter her door. Grief fell upon her weary shoulders with a weight she thought she could not bear. Now there was only the slow, tortured passing of time before she would learn the heartbreaking truth.

All through the night the search went on. Then, at dawn, a shout rang out through the swamp. "Look!" a man shouted. "Somethin' is floatin' in the water, over there, by the cypress log." The rising sun was breaking through the clouds in a violet sky. By its golden rays, they saw something black and shiny floating gently on the glittering water. They slowly guided their *pirogues* through the maze of rotten timbers jutting from the water. With trembling hands, they grasped fistfuls of the long hair and pulled until they freed the pale lifeless body of Rapadeen.

The sun was still low in the east when the men returned. Mama Marie stood on the *galerie* and watched them lift the girl from the *pirogue*. "Rapadeen?" she asked softly, and waited in fearful silence for their answer. Then the words came, striking her down like lightning. "Marie, your girl is gone. Rapadeen is dead."

For two days the men worked to make a vault for the girl. Mama and the women prepared the body for burial. They dressed the girl in a white gown and spread her long curling hair over her shoulders. They placed the girl's hands gently across her still bosom and covered her eyes with silver dollars.

The evening of the second day Rapadeen was laid to rest in a little family cemetery among the vaults of her ancestors. On the third day Mama planted velvety red roses around the girl's vault. As she worked, her teardrops fell on the flowers and glistened like morning dew.

Marie mourned her daughter with a terrible sorrow sharpened by regret. If only she could undo the past and take back her angry words. If only she could tell her *'tite fille* how much Mama loved her. A cold wind raged through her soul, and she clung to her grief like a lifeline.

A year passed—a year to the day of Rapadeen's death. That night Marie lay in bed, remembering and weeping. She missed her daughter now more than ever. The mother prayed with all her soul for tender mercy. "*Mon Bon Dieu,*" she begged silently, "please hear my prayer. Tell Rapadeen I love her. Give me a sign she knows. I cannot let my girl go and I cannot keep on livin' until there is peace between us."

At last sweet sleep came and softened her pain. She slept deeply and dreamed Rapadeen was there with her. Mother and daughter lovingly embraced one another as each forgave and was forgiven. Then the girl was drifting away, light as dandelion fluff on a summer breeze. Marie pleaded with her to stay, but she only shook her head. "Don't be afraid Mama," she said. "We'll be together again." Giving her mama a little smile, Rapadeen waved good-bye and was gone.

Mama Marie waked with a start. Was it true? Had

Rapadeen really been there? Was it a sign from heaven or just a dream? She tried to believe *Le Bon Dieu* answered her prayer, but her faith was only a small flickering flame in the great dark night. She lay quietly, listening to the lonesome song of the swamp, when suddenly she heard unfamiliar sounds coming from the cook room.

Marie sat up in bed and listened. Yes, someone was out there. There was a low clatter of plates being laid down, as though someone was setting the table. Thinking it must be her son, she called out softly, "Guillaume, is that you?" The chirping of the crickets was her only reply.

Her hands were shaking as she lit the kerosene lamp beside her bed and turned the light down low. Slowly, slowly she walked bare-footed to the lean-to at the back of the *cabane*. She entered the door and gasped. Someone had come in the night and set the table all nice, just like company was coming. But who?

Suddenly the room filled with the sweet perfume of flowers. The woman raised her dim lamp high and cried out. There in the center of the table lay a big bouquet of blood-red roses. Marie knew her prayers had been answered. Even if only for a moment, Rapadeen had returned to give her Mama a sign. Now, at last, mother and daughter were at peace.

Marie lived long enough to see her son grow to manhood. When it came her time to depart this world, she passed through the veil lightly, for she knew Rapadeen would be waiting for her somewhere on the other side.

Since that time, mother and daughter reunite once a

year in their old *cabane* to laugh and talk together in perfect peace. There are some who say the tale of Marie and Rapadeen is only foolish superstition. But the old ones believe, for they have seen many strange happenings in their time. Perhaps they know better than anyone that nothing, not even death, can kill a mother's love. But only the Great Basin herself knows the true story, and she's not telling.

The Ghost of Jean Lafitte

Down below New Orleans, the land melts into the salt marshlands of Barataria. It was there among the chênières—*the high mounds of shells covered with live oak trees*—*that Jean Lafitte, the pirate, plied his trade. He made the greatest part of his fortune from the sale of seized human cargoes*—*African slaves. Legend has it that Lafitte buried his riches and never returned to claim his ill-gotten gain. Countless treasure seekers have dug up Louisiana from New Orleans to the Sabine River looking for the pirate's long lost riches. This old tale is the only clue to the treasure's location. But treasure hunters beware*—*the treasure of Jean Lafitte is forever cursed.*

A young, war-weary Confederate soldier was making his long way back home, following the snaking path of a bayou, when a terrible storm fell upon him. The wind wailed as thunder boomed and rain fell like needles. The soldier saw that he had better find shelter, so he left the bayou and began to wander through a thicket. He soon became lost in the blinding rain.

The soldier came to an abandoned house in the middle of nowhere. The door stood open. He called out but nobody answered, and since it was nearly dark, he went inside to escape the howling wind. He struck a match and found dry firewood left behind by some other lost soul. The young man quickly made a fire and settled down for the night. He was dead tired from his journey, and he soon fell into a heavy sleep.

Sometime in the deep of the night he waked with the strange feeling that he was not alone in the house. And there by the light of the dying fire, he saw the ghostly figure of a man standing in tall, muddy boots. His arms were folded across his chest, and a pirate's cutlass hung at his side.

The man pointed at him and moaned, "Come with me."

"Who—who are you?" whispered the soldier.

"I am Jean Lafitte," he wailed. *"Viens avec moi!* Come with me. Save my soul. Help me!"

The man disappeared into thin air without another word. The soldier's heart was pounding, but he told himself it was only a dream. He stoked the fire and lay back down. The apparition had unsettled him, and now he jumped at every creak and groan of the old house, until at last his tired body gave in to sleep.

The fire had died down when the soldier again waked with a start. An icy draft of wind whistled through the room, and the ghostly pirate appeared once more before him.

"Help me, free my soul," the pirate's spirit pleaded.

The young man could barely speak for fear. "Wh—what do you wa—want from m—me?" he gasped.

"I am condemned," wailed the ghost, "a slave to my

treasure, bought with human tears and broken hearts. Now I must pay the price of my fortune. My soul is bound to my blood money. Take my treasure and set me freeeee!"

The young man could feel himself being lifted against his will and forced to follow the ghost of Jean Lafitte. The spirit brought him to a secret room. There, with a wave of the pirate's hand, the boards in the floor disappeared to reveal a huge chest, spilling over with treasure. The room was lit up by the glow of silver, jewels, and golden coins.

Jean Lafitte stretched out his hands, crying, "Take it! Take my treasure. Save my soul!"

The spirit's hands were gory, and bloody tears dripped from his burning eyes. He reached out, closer, closer, until the young man felt the bloodstained fingers grasp his arm like an icy claw—it was the touch of death itself. The soldier's terror rose beyond the power of the spirit's spell and he broke away, running like a madman into the stormy night. The wind tore at him and booming thunder shook the ground. He crashed through the thorny thicket in the blinding rain. Behind him he could hear the ghost crying in the wind, "Take my treasure. Ohhhhh, help meee!"

The young man lived to tell the story, and he warned all who would seek the treasure to beware. The pirate's bloody curse, he would say, follows whoever takes the treasure. To this day, when a storm booms down the bayou, the wailing wind carries the pitiful cries of the ghost of Jean Lafitte. His spirit is condemned to wander forever through the dark night, begging, pleading for somebody to take his cursed treasure and free his tortured soul at last.

The Spirit that
Would Not Be Tamed

Some old-time Cajun treasure hunters believed a fifolet
*light could lead them to treasure, which was often guarded
by a spirit. Jean Lafitte, the pirate, was said to have killed
a man for each cache of treasure and buried him alongside
the ill-got booty. Faithful even in death, this murdered
mate stands watch, ready to defend the pirate's gold.
Treasure hunters who encountered this force from beyond
sometimes hired a spirit tamer, whose supernatural
powers subdued the treasure-guarding ghosts. Here is a
new story based on an old tradition, told with a twist of
Cajun humor.*

Delmer B. Gulley sat in the hot July sun studying the
fork in the dirt road, pondering which way he ought
to go. His feet were killing him, and he was about to roast
inside the sober black suit and tight reverend's collar he
was wearing. Pulling a grimy handkerchief out of his
otherwise empty britches pocket, he mopped his face and
sighed deeply over his recent stroke of bad luck. Here he
was, lost in some Louisiana swamp hole, swatting
mosquitoes, without a nickel to his name.

Still, it could have been worse. It was a good thing that freight train pulled out when it did. If he hadn't jumped in an empty boxcar and got across the river quick, that bunch on the Texas side would have taken a chunk out of his hide for true.

It was a downright shame, too. Everything was going just fine. Then that nosy biddy found out that the Reverend Delmer B. Gulley's Miracle Tonic, guaranteed to cure everything from Asthma to Yellow Fever, was nothing but watered-down cod liver oil flavored with a shot of cheap whiskey.

Mrs. Bertha Hebert had purchased a big bottle of Miracle Tonic and swallowed down a large dose to relieve her irritated sciatic nerve. It was then that she discovered the one and only thing it could cure. After trotting back and forth to the outhouse all day, she ran to the sheriff crying foul play.

It was just his luck that Bertha Hebert was the wife of Big Jack Hebert, the sheriff. Not only did the sheriff confiscate all his Miracle Tonic profits, but he promised to tar and feather the phony Reverend Delmer B. Gulley, common con man and petty thief, if he did not hightail it out of town by sundown.

Common con man indeed, he thought. *That two-bit, one-horse-town sheriff don't know talent when he sees it. I am a con artist, a master of disguise.*

Delmer B. Gulley took great pride in his career of crime. With a change of clothing he had transformed himself into an colonel, a banker, and the owner of a

Nevada gold mine. He had once even passed himself off as Lord Delmer, Duke of Gulley.

Yes siree, I've pulled off some capers in my time, he thought, cheering a little. *This here's a minor setback. My luck is bound to change and I'll be in tall clover again.* Delmer brushed the dust off his lapel and looked unhappily at the fork in the road. He was deep in thought, considering all the angles of his miserable situation, when he heard a wagon approaching.

Delmer ducked behind a tree. In his line of business he had learned it paid to be cautious. Soon the wagon rounded the bend. Two men in wide-brimmed straw hats sat atop a rattletrap wagon, driving an old bag o' bones mule. Delmer peeped out from behind the tree. *Aha*, he thought, *just a couple of local fellas.* He straightened his reverend's collar and assumed a pious expression. *I have a feeling I'm about to be rescued.*

The Rev. Delmer B. Gulley stepped into the dirt lane and hailed the men. They pulled to a stop and stared with interest at the skinny stranger in the heavy black coat. "Good afternoon, gentlemen," he said. "Allow me to introduce myself. I am the Reverend Delmer B. Gulley, a poor wandering preacher new to these parts. I'm afraid I have got myself lost. Could you fellas point me towards the nearest town?"

The two men exchanged glances. "*M'sieur*," the smaller man said, "you are lost I guarantee. There is no town the way you are goin'. You gotta go up this road, mebbe seven, six mile and cross the train track. Follow that road, it is straight all the way. You gonna find the village on Bayou Chinquapin."

Delmer had no intention of walking his aching dogs all the way back down that hot dusty road. With the natural ease of a born liar, he quickly concocted a slick story sure to win over these bumpkins. He shook his head sadly. "Yes," he said, "I know about the train track. It was there I met my demise."

"Well, your Demise should not have left you way out here. But, that is just like them womenfolk will do a man," the little man added sympathetically.

"Er, no," Delmer said, "I mean to say, that is where I had my trouble. You see, being a poor preacher who depends on the charity of my brothers, I could not afford a ticket. So, I was forced to borrow a lift in a boxcar. But I was not alone. A great big fella was crouchin' in the corner. He demanded my money. When he found out I didn't have a plug nickel to my name, he threatened to carve me with his initials. Naturally, I had to jump for my life," he said dramatically. "I dare not return to the tracks. Why, that fiend is probably hid out right now, just waitin' for me to mosey down the road."

Delmer looked from face to face. The short man and his huge companion clearly believed his tale. "So as you can see, I could surely use a hand in gettin' out of here, Mr., er, what did you say your names were?"

The two men looked at each other and the big one nodded. "Me, I am Alphonse Theriot and this is my brother Alcide," said the small man pointing to the silent giant of a man that sat beside him. "We can give you a ride to Bayou Chinquapin, *mais sho'*. Nobody gonna mess with us, *M'sieur*. You gonna be plenty safe, but we best be gettin' on before dark."

Delmer wasted no time in swinging his dusty valise into the wagon and jumping in himself. He was curious to see it was loaded with lanterns, shovels, rope and a hefty pickax. "If I didn't know better," he said, grinning like a Chessie cat, "I'd swear you fellas were minin' for gold out in that swamp."

The brothers swung around and stared at him. "*M'sieur*, why do you say that?" Alphonse demanded. "What does a preacher man know about diggin' for gold?"

"Well sir," Delmer said, sizing up the two men, "my work has led me all over this great land. It just so happens, I once rescued a fella who owned a gold mine in Nevada."

"You say you rescued him? From what, *M'sieur*?" Alphonse asked curiously.

Delmer could see he really had these fellas going. He stifled a guffaw and lied earnestly, "Why, I saved his mortal soul is all! It weren't no easy thing either, believe you me. That fella was just about to strike it rich when a mean ol' demon spirit got into the mine and just ruined everything. Sure shootin', that devil pestered that fella every time he set foot in his mine. Throwed rocks, smashed his lanterns, even stole his gold! Yes sir, the devil spirit took over the mine and was aimin' to get his claws in that fella too." Delmer paused and let the weight of this sink in on the Theriot brothers. "Luckily," he said modestly, "I was able to rescue the poor fella and run that devil right out of his gold mine."

The two men looked at the Reverend Delmer B. Gulley with considerable respect. "What did ya do to get rid of that bad spirit?" Alphonse asked eagerly.

"Why, I relied on The Good Book," Delmer said pulling out a worn, red-leather-bound copy of *The Gentleman's Guide to Poker*. He slammed his hand down over the title. "Here's how I done it!" he declared. "I preached that bad ol' spirit back to Hades. Whupped up on him with The Word. You know," Delmer said confidentially, "there's not many can look a devil in the eye and not flinch a muscle."

The Theriot brothers looked long and hard at each other. At last Alcide gave his brother a silent nod of approval. "My brother wants I should tell you our little secret," Alphonse said mysteriously. "You bein' a preacherman and all, we figure we can trust you. Mebbe you are just the man to help us." Alphonse looked up and down the path. Although the road was deserted, he lowered his voice. "You see, *M'sieur*, you are right. Me and Alcide are diggin' for gold in the swamp. We are treasure hunters and we have found the hidden buried gold of Jean Lafitte."

"What?" Delmer asked, "You say you found a treasure?"

The two brothers nodded together. *"Mais oui, M'sieur!"* Alphonse exclaimed. "It was a *fifolet* that led us to it. For a year we tracked that spirit through the swamp woods until, at last, he could trick us no more. And me and

Alphonse, WE FOUND IT!" The silent Alcide nodded his huge head excitedly.

"We have seen it with our own eyes for true," Alphonse continued. "It is a huge chest filled with a *beaucoup* of gold and silver coins. We dug it up two times already. But we can't get it outta the ground, *M'sieur*," he said, leaning closer to Delmer. "The treasure is guarded by a bad spirit. Every time we dig it up, that ghost just jumps on us so, it scares the daylights out of us. We holler and that treasure sinks deeper into the ground. That bad ol' ghost beats us with sticks and rocks until we cannot help but run away, howlin' like whupped dogs!"

Delmer couldn't believe his ears. He'd heard of Cajuns and their superstitions, but maybe these fellas were just pulling his leg. *Could be they're givin' me a taste of my own medicine*, Delmer thought, *or, maybe they are tellin' the truth. If they have found some money, it could be that my luck is about to change. All that talk about bad spirits don't amount to nothin'. Why, they prob'ly scared themselves out there in the swamp, thinkin' there was a ghost after them. Well, there's only one way to find out.*

"I see your problem," Delmer said thoughtfully. "Of course you can trust me, but what can I do to help you fellas get the treasure?"

"M'sieur Gulley, it is plain to me and Alcide that you are a spirit tamer," Alphonse said breathlessly. "All you got to do is tame that ol' ghost long enough so that he can't scare me and Alcide so bad. Then, while you are keepin' that spirit tamed down, me and my brother can dig up the gold. Once it's in our hands, it is ours. No ghost is gonna get it back then, I guarantee!"

"Now boys, I reckon I could tame that spirit for you all right," Delmer said with a greedy gleam in his eyes. "But spirit tamin' is real dangerous work. I don't suppose ya'll would ask a fella to risk his life for nothin'? Mind ya, I ain't askin' for myself, but a generous love offerin' from you fellas would surely help me carry on my work. Now, what I had in mind was a share in that there treasure, an equal share. And if it turns out there ain't no treasure," Delmer said, "I'd still get a little somethin' for my time, say a hundred dollars."

The two brothers looked at each other, and after a lively exchange of frowns and gestures, Alcide gave his nod of approval. "My brother don't like cuttin' you in for a third of the treasure," said Alphonse, "but he reckons we won't get the treasure at all if we don't hire a spirit tamer."

Delmer was eager to get started. The sooner he tamed that spirit the sooner he would get paid. Of course, there really was no such thing as ghosts at all, but if the Theriot brothers wanted to believe in spirits, that was fine with him. He'd put on a real good show for those fellas. By the time he got through they would believe that the Reverend Delmer B. Gulley, part-time spirit tamer, had really chased away that bad ol' ghost for good.

The deal was struck and Delmer shook hands with Alphonse and Alcide to seal the bargain. They decided to dig up the loot that very night. There was no time to delay. Some other treasure hunter might discover where the gold was buried, get their own spirit tamer, and snatch the treasure out from under their noses.

After supper the men headed out to claim their treasure. Alcide pulled the wagon to a stop where the dirt path dead-ended at the edge of the swamp. "Here's where we get out and walk, M'sieur Gulley," Alphonse said in a hushed voice. "C'mon now, and whatever you do, be quiet. We don't want that spirit to get the jump on you!"

Delmer followed the Theriot brothers through the swamp woods. In the half-dark the shadowy cypress trees silently watched their every move, while off in the distance the sudden cry of a screech owl sent a shiver down his spine. It seemed to him that the mosquitoes whining in his ear were warning him to get away. *Aw, those Cajuns and their ghost stories have got my nerves on edge*, he thought. *I gotta quit thinkin' about spirits and keep my mind on gettin' my just rewards outta this deal.*

The three men walked deeper into the swampwoods until the Theriot brothers came to an abrupt halt. "What are we doin'?" Delmer asked in a whisper.

"We're waitin,'" Alphonse whispered back in reply.

"Well," Delmer asked, raising his voice impatiently, "what're we waitin' for?"

"Shhh! We are waitin' to be sure the *fifolet* is gone!"

Suddenly, away off in the swampwoods, Delmer saw a strange, shimmering blue light appear out of the thin air. It hovered for a moment at the roots of an ancient forked cypress tree, then floated away and disappeared into the growing darkness. Delmer's eyes bugged out at the sight.

"What in tarnation was that?" he demanded.

"Shhh!" whispered Alphonse. "That was the *fifolet!* It is good he is gone. The *fifolet* tempts you to follow him, but that is very dangerous. He tries to lead you to water, and then he does his best to make you drown. Sometimes a *fifolet* will lead you to treasure. But there is no time for talk now. We must go dig for the treasure before the *fifolet* returns. We do not want you to tame two spirits."

"What are you talkin' about?" Delmer asked in alarm. "Two spirits?"

"M'sieur Gulley, the *fifolet* led us to the treasure," Alphonse whispered, "but the gold is guarded by a bad ghost. That is the spirit you have got to tame for true. Reverend, you best get ready now in case that ol' ghost swoops down on us. C'mon, grab some tools, and let's go get to diggin'."

Delmer did not like this sudden turn of events. He had come along with the certainty that there was no such thing as ghosts. Now he wasn't so sure. *Oh, get a grip on yourself, Gulley,* he told himself angrily. *That fifolet ain't nothin' but swamp gas. There's nothin' to worry about.*

The three men picked their way silently through the undergrowth to the forked cypress. "This is the spot," Alphonse said softly, pointing to the soggy ground at the base of the cypress tree. "Stand back, preacher. Alcide can bust through to the treasure a lot quicker than you and me. I'll help my brother. You just be ready to tame that spirit. By the way, where is your Good Book? You said that was how you was gonna whup that bad ghost."

Delmer smiled feebly and patted *The Gentleman's Guide to Poker* in his deep coat pocket. Alcide lit the lantern and turned its light down to a dull glow. He lifted the pickax and began breaking ground. With each blow of the pickax, Delmer relaxed. It was just as he thought. There wasn't any ghost at all, just a little swamp gas and a couple of fellas with wild imaginations.

Suddenly, Alcide's pickax struck against something with a hollow thud. The two men grabbed shovels and quickly dug, revealing an old-fashioned trunk. Delmer held his breath as the two brothers carefully worked ropes under the chest and heaved it out of the hole. Alcide pried the trunk open and held the dim lantern close to look at its contents.

Delmer couldn't believe it. The Theriot men had told the truth. They really had found a treasure! Inside the chest, hundreds of golden coins shined in the lantern light. It was too good to be true. He, Delmer B. Gulley, was now a rich man. A third of that treasure belonged to him. At long last his luck had changed. *This is the best job I've ever pulled off,* he thought gleefully. *Who says crime don't pay? Yes sir, I might just take up spirit tamin' permanently.*

He stood back congratulating himself on his brilliant work and secretly laughing at the silly Theriot brothers. They had cut him in for a third of the treasure, and all because they were scared of spirits. *Serves 'em right,* Delmer thought. *After all, everbody knows there's no such thing as ghosts—*

"AAAIIIEEHH!" Out of the blue, Alcide howled loud

enough to wake the dead. "YEEOOOWWW!" Alphonse screeched, "It's got us, Gulley. It's beatin' us to pieces!" The two men were hollering and jumping as a stick wielded by an unseen hand thrashed them. Delmer longed to sprint from the place, but his feet were frozen to the ground. He would have screamed too, but his tongue hung thick and heavy in his mouth.

Alphonse was hollering with pain while his huge brother, Alcide, whimpered like a baby. "Gulley, ya gotta do somethin'," Alphonse yelled. "If you don't tame that spirit real quick, we're gonna lose all that gold!"

The mention of losing his near wealth, brought Delmer back to life. He felt the weight of his Good Book in his pocket. *Well,* Delmer thought, *I've tricked plenty of folks in my time, dumb and smart alike. I bet I can trick this ol' ghost too. One thing is for sure, I ain't givin' up that gold without a fight.*

The Reverend Gulley whipped out his red-leather poker guide. It fell open to Lesson Number Two: "The winning poker player never reveals his true thoughts to his opponent." He said to himself, *I can bluff that spirit, sure I can. I'll send him flyin' back to Purgatory all right!* Delmer mastered his knocking knees and drew a deep breath. He fixed his face into a stony mask and steeled his nerves for the best performance of his entire con artist career.

"Spirit of the treasure, your day of reckonin' has come. I am here to tame you once and for all. I COMMAND you to stop beatin' those fellas now," he roared, "or I, the

Reverend Delmer B. Gulley, am gonna WHUP YOU!"

All at once, the stick dropped and a hush fell. "You did it, M'sieur Gulley," Alphonse exclaimed, "You chased that ol' ghost away for true. You are some good spirit tamer, I guarantee!" Delmer secretly breathed a sigh of relief.

"Yep," he said swaggering, "I knew I could tame that spirit all right. Why, there isn't a ghost around I can't whup. Of course, a bad ghost like that is naturally scared of The Word. It's easy to see that spirit knew what was good for him. Too bad he didn't stick around a little longer though," Gulley bragged, "or you would've seen a real fight."

Delmer was running his fingers through the gold imagining how he was going to spend his share, when wild laughter suddenly filled the night. "HEE-HEE-HEE-HEE! Thought ya got rid of me, didn't ya, Gulley?" a shrill voice teased. "But I'm not done yet. You like a good fight, eh? Well then, spirit tamer, get to it. Just how do you think you're gonna tame me?"

Delmer swallowed hard. "Ghost, I'm gonna whup you with The Word, straight out of the Good Book," he managed to squeak. "Yes siree bob, I got all the weapons I need right here!" Delmer pulled out *The Gentleman's Guide* and shook it at the thin air.

"We'll just see about that, preacher!" the ghost hissed.

To his horror, Delmer saw the big stick swinging towards him, a split-second away from putting a knot on his head. In his panic he remembered the book in his hand.

Quick as lightning he raised up *The Gentleman's Guide to Poker* and put it between the big stick and his own tender noggin. WHAMM! The stick struck the book with vicious force and sent it hurtling to the ground.

All of a sudden, Delmer heard wild laughter behind him. An invisible icy hand tapped him on the shoulder. "HEE-HEE-HEE-HEE, here I am," the spirit whined. "Now, I'm waitin' to hear how you're gonna whup me … saaay, wait just one minute … well, would ya look at that? Why, that ain't the Good Book at all! You got a lot of gall threatening me with a lousy poker book. If there is one thing I can't stand worse than a preacher, it's a cotton-rotten-hunk-of-skunk phony preacher! Reverend, you have played your last card," the spook wailed. "I'll teach you not to trick a poor ol' ghost who can't help but guard his treasure. You better run, Gulley, 'cause I'm going to teach you a lesson you'll never forget!"

Delmer's feet took off running before the rest of him did, giving him a big disadvantage in a race with a ghost. He had hardly run three steps when the ghost walloped him across his backside with *The Gentleman's Guide to Poker*. Alcide and Alphonse watched in amazement as Delmer yelped like a beat dog and bolted. He was moving faster than a jackrabbit on fire trying to outrun the ghost, who was thoroughly trouncing him with the battered poker book.

The Theriot brothers could still hear Delmer, hollering off in the distance as they loaded up the treasure chest in their wagon. By the time they'd driven their mule up to the tracks, Delmer was long gone. The only trace they found of the skinny con man was his red-leather-bound copy of *The Gentleman's Guide to Poker.* Mysteriously, its pages were turned to Lesson Number One: "In poker, as in life, a winner never underestimates his opponent."

"Yeah, that is some good advice for true," Alphonse said. "It is too bad M'sieur Gulley skipped that Lesson Number One. He would've known better than to try and tame a spirit with nothin' but pure-dee bluff." His huge brother Alcide nodded silently in wise agreement.

Nobody ever met up with the Reverend Delmer B. Gulley or the ghost again. Alcide and Alphonse had their treasure at last. Figuring a deal was a deal, they watched over Delmer's share for many a year. When at last it was clear he was never coming back to Bayou Chinquapin, they donated his gold to The Home for Wayward Boys down in New Orleans. They thought that Delmer would have wanted it that way.

For years and years folks argued over the fate of Delmer B. Gulley. Some say he jumped a train and got away—after all, he was one slick con man. But the Theriot brothers had a different idea. Since the ghost no longer had a treasure to guard and nothing better to do, they figured it chased him right out of this world and into the next one. Best as they can tell, Delmer B. Gulley is still running, and you can bet that ol' ghost is right on his heels.

Why Onions Make Us Cry

I once met a man who told me this story for true. An old Cajun man became stranded in Kansas. He went to work for a farmer but he was homesick. Before long he fell ill and lay on his deathbed. The old man begged for onions but the farmer refused his request. The Cajun man soon died. My acquaintance, a farm boy at the time, found the fella's special onion knife. He swears that when he picked up the knife, it crumbled in his hand and disappeared. From this account I wove a ghostly pourquoi *tale dedicated to the memory of that old Cajun man who died far from home, his dying wish unfulfilled.*

Most of the folks who lived along Bayou LaFourche figured Z'Onion Joe must be crazy. After all, who but a crazy man would live all alone, deep in the shadowy swamp on a rickety shantyboat? He was odd-looking enough with that long white beard flowing down his chest and his bright black eyes peering out from beneath bushy gray brows. A floppy, beat-up hat was always pulled down low over his greasy wisps of mossy hair, and a patchwork of rags covered his lean, bony frame.

People joked that Z'Onion Joe had lived alone with the wild things for so long that he was half alligator and moon-mad to boot. But to some folks, Z'Onion Joe was no laughing matter. Why, he might be some kind of a wizard who'd work a *gris-gris* on you if you made him mad. So while most of the bayou people poked fun at the old man, others crossed themselves and spat when they saw him coming. Suspicious Mamas warned their children to keep out of his way. "Be good," they'd say, "or Z'Onion Joe will getcha and carry ya away!"

Stranger still was the old man's habits. When he did make a rare appearance in the village, he never visited over a cup of *café au lait*, but straight away traded a huge fresh *goujon* or muskrat pelt for dozens of big yellow onions. Then, taking the great burlap sack which always hung from his shoulder, he filled it to the top with the onions until the heavy bag dragged on the ground. "So many *z'onions!*" the people whispered. "What could a man do with so many *z'onions?*"

Of course, everybody along the bayou flavored their gumbos with onions, but nobody loved onions like that old man. Since he had mysteriously appeared over eighty years before, that hermit had roamed the bayou trading with the LaFourche folks. They reckoned that he had to be at least a hundred years old, maybe even older. But his back was still as strong as a cypress tree, and he could work as hard as any young man.

He claimed that eating all those onions gave him his youth and strength. He ate onions every meal—boiled, fried, roasted, and raw. Whenever he got sick, he just pressed the juice from an onion, mixed it with a few drops of turpentine to taste, and that potion would fix him right up. He even had a special prized onion knife that was his most beloved possession. For true, he loved onions so much that everybody up and down the bayou called him Z'Onion Joe.

Now, anybody who ate dozens of onions every day should have been smellin' to high heaven and red-eyed from those strong, stinging onion fumes. But believe it or not, a long, long time ago, *z'onions* did not have that awful burning odor. *Mais non!* Back in those days, onions were just sweet and full of delicious flavor. Z'Onion Joe loved them the way a baby loves milk. As long as he could barter for all the onions he wanted, he was a happy, satisfied man.

But one spring a terrible *malheur* came over the land. Day after day the sun blazed down until the earth was parched and cracked. The drought dried up the wells. Tender seedlings wilted in the narrow ribbon gardens that stretched from the hand-built levees of the bayou to the outback. At last, in July, a warm rain began to fall and the people rejoiced. The drought was broken! Perhaps something could be saved yet of the gardens they had worked so hard to plant.

But after many days of rain, their joy turned to despair. It seemed that the sky itself was falling. Such rain they had never seen; it rained and rained until the swollen rivers and bayous spilled over their banks, pouring torrents of water across the land. It rained until whole villages were forced to flee. All along the bayou, people packed up their meager supply of food and possessions and headed north for higher ground.

Miles away, deep within the swamp, Z'Onion Joe was riding out the flood in his makeshift shantyboat. For him, the rising water held riches. Scraps of lumber, fish nets, a wooden bucket, and a perfectly good three-legged pegged chair washed right up to his front door. The old man fished the treasures from the water with a big grin. Why, there was enough scrap to keep his houseboat floating forever and plenty of junk to trade for his beloved onions. *Any day now,* he thought, *it'll quit rainin' and I'll go get me some more z'onions.* But the rain kept coming down until at last the hermit was down to his last dozen onions.

Z'Onion Joe set off in his *pirogue* to barter for more *z'onions.* He traveled up and down the bayou through the rain, but all he found was flooded, empty villages. There was not an onion to be found anywhere on Bayou LaFourche for love or money. It nearly broke his heart to leave the wild beauty and quiet peace of the swamp, but there was nothing else to do. Z'Onion Joe turned his *pirogue* around and headed north in search of onions.

He traveled by water for three days until he reached soggy but solid ground. The hermit tied up his *pirogue*, hiding it well in some undergrowth, and set out on foot. At last, footsore and weary, he found himself passing by a run-down farm sitting off a lonely dirt path. The old man's onion supply had run out, and he was feeling mighty weak. He was desperate to get his hands on some onions. Z'Onion Joe walked up to the farmhouse door and knocked.

After a few moments the door swung open. A sharp faced woman with a nose like the beak of a bird poked her head out and eyed the stranger with suspicion. "What do ya want?" she demanded. "If you're sellin', we ain't buyin'!"

Z'Onion Joe took off his greasy hat and spoke, "*Comment ça va, Madame?* I am looking for work. I am old, but me, I can still work plenty hard. Just you give me a try and see if I do not speak the truth."

By this time the woman's husband had joined her at the door. He was an ugly man with beady, greedy eyes and an angry scowl on his face. "What's this ol' fool want?" he asked, hooking his thumb in the direction of the old man. "Says he wants work," his wife whispered. "Claims he's a hard worker. Reckon he must be one of them folks runnin' from that bad floodin' down south."

"Hmmmm," said the farmer looking Z'Onion Joe over. "I could use a hand, but I ain't got the money to pay any ol' shiftless bum come beggin' around my place! Me? Hire an ol' man like you? Why, you'd prob'ly eat more than you'd work."

Z'Onion Joe looked around the place. Suddenly his eyes lit on a heap of burlap bags. "What did ya say ya'll farm?" he asked.

The farmer's greedy eyes narrowed. "A little of this, a little of that. Run a few head of cattle, got some fields in cotton, some in cane, and of course we grow our own stuff: beans, corn, peppers, and ... onions."

Z'Onion Joe's dark eyes brightened. The thought of

onions made his mouth water. "Well," he said, stroking his long white beard, "how 'bout if I work for ya'll for nothin'? That's right, me, I'll work, but you don't have to pay me a single cent. Just fill me up one of them totebags over there with *z'onions*. That's all I want. Just give me all the *z'onions* I can eat and I'll be a happy man.

The farmer and his wife exchanged a sly look. So, this foolish old man was willing to work for onions. He looked strong enough, and after all, what were a few onions? An extra pair of hands and a strong back would mean more crops, and more money to add to their carefully hidden stash of gold coins. Although their place looked run down, the truth was the farmer and his wife were misers. They were too stingy to spend any of their secret gold on keeping their farm up.

At night the wife closed the shutters tight and barred the door while her husband brought out the chest that held their riches. By candle light the two of them counted their precious gold. They loved their money more than anything else in the world. Now this crazy man had come along and offered to help them make even more money—and all for a few onions. It was too good to be true!

The farmer pretended to think the offer over. "Well," he said at last, "I s'pose I'm just too soft-hearted for my own good, but I reckon I'll take a chance on you. What did ya say your name was?"

"Most folks call me Z'Onion Joe down on the bayou," said the old man, "on account of how I love to eat *z'onions*."

"Well, Z'Onion Joe," said the farmer, "you'll sleep in the barn. You can fetch yourself a couple dozen onions now, but here on out, payday is Friday. Come around then and fill up your bag, but don't think I'm not countin' those onions! Old man or not, we made a deal and I expect a hard day's work outta you! You might as well go ahead and get started workin off your first bag of onions."

That night the farmer and his wife counted their precious gold and gloated over the shrewd deal they had made. But when the couple retired to bed, their sleep was troubled. Their stash of secret gold brought them no peace or contentment.

As they tossed and turned, plotting in their dreams how they might hoard even more money, Z'Onion Joe sharpened up his special knife and prepared to celebrate his own good luck with a feast. But before his knife cut into a single sweet onion, the old man bowed his head and gave thanks to *Le Bon Dieu* for the bounty of His blessings. Then Z'Onion Joe savored each sweet, delicious mouthful of onion. His hunger satisfied, he fell asleep a happy man.

Weeks passed and everything was going along smoothly. The farmer and his wife had a fine worker for a cheap price, and Z'Onion Joe had all the sweet onions he could eat. But the couple soon began to wonder if they had made such a good deal after all. Being naturally greedy themselves, they just couldn't believe that the old man didn't care for money. How could he be so happy and satisfied when he was poor as a churchmouse? Why didn't Z'Onion Joe want to be paid in money like everybody else?

One night the farmer and his wife sat in their rocking chairs counting their hoard of golden coins by candlelight. The reflection of the flickering flame gleamed in their eyes. Eerie shadows played on their faces, twisting their sharp features into grotesque masks. The coins shined and clanked in their cold, eager hands, but the gold brought them no pleasure. Each squeak of their chairs seemed to nag at them, *Why? Why? Why doesn't the ol' man want money?* Every creak groaned, *Why? Why? Why does the ol' man want onions? Squeak, creak, nag, groan, Why, Why, WHY?* Their selfish minds stewed and simmered with curiosity until suspicion bubbled up and their outrage spilled over.

The farmer jumped up out of his chair, sending a lapful of coins clattering to the floor. His red face was contorted with rage. "I tell you there's a rat in the corn crib," he shouted. "All Z'Onion Joe wants is onions, onions, and more onions. There's gotta be some hidden, secret wealth in them onions, and we been givin' it all away to that crazy ol' man. I tell ya he's been cheatin' us out of a fortune!"

The sharp-beaked woman stared at her husband. "What are you jabberin' about? What treasure could there be in them onions? That ol' fella ain't got nothin' but his onion knife to his name, unless you count his good health. Just imagine, he must be over a hundred years old, and he's the healthiest, strongest man I've ever seen. Why, he can work circles 'round you! You'd think he'd be all tired and broken down, but no! It's like he's got some kind of magic, like he knows some secret."

All of a sudden the woman screamed, "That's it! Don't you see? Z'Onion Joe has discovered the secret of eternal youth! He knows how to live forever! It's all in them onions—and we been givin' them all away!"

The farmer pounded the table with his fist. "Woman, for once you are right! But the magic must be more than just the onions. He must know some kind of a spell. I betcha he's got a *gris-gris* charm too!" The greedy husband and wife shared the same thought. "The knife!" they shouted. "The magic must be in his onion knife!"

All night long the couple schemed until they had a plan. They would find out the secret for true. Tomorrow was Friday and that wizard would come around to claim his bag of onions. But not one onion would they give that old man. "Come in," they would say, "we have your onions inside." Then they would shove him into a store room and lock him up. He would tell them his magic spell and hand over that charmed knife, or he would starve to death and carry his secret to the grave.

The next evening Z'Onion Joe finished up his work at sundown. He gathered up a tote bag and went up to the house to collect his onions. The farmer and his wife had been watching and waiting all evening for their prey to arrive. When at last the old man knocked, they gave each other a knowing nod and rushed to open the door.

"*Bon soir, Madame,*" said Z'Onion Joe. "I have come for my onions and to tell you that I will take my leave tomorrow. You have been good to give me work, but I am a man of the swamp. It is time for me to return home."

"So you will leave in the morning," said the wife with a wicked smile. "Then you must come inside and spend your last night with us. Your onions are in the storeroom, the best of our last harvest. Come in and we will fill your bag. Join us for supper and a good rest in a soft bed. When you wake in the morning, your bag will be full, and I will send you off with a good breakfast and a cup of hot coffee!"

Z'Onion Joe hesitated, for he did not like to sleep in a house. It made him feel restless, like a caged animal. "*Merci beaucoup, Madame*," he said, "but I will be up and gone before the sunrise. I would not want to be any trouble to you. I will just get my *z'onions* now and be on my way back to the barn."

The woman's smile turned to a sneer. Seeing his wife had failed to trick the old man into staying the night, the farmer took matters in his own hands. "All right then," he growled, "come on and get your onions. You're holdin' up our supper. Bring your bag and follow me!"

Z'Onion Joe followed the farmer deeper and deeper into the sprawling farmhouse. At last the farmer stopped before a locked door at the end of a long dark hall. The man unlocked the door and pushed it open.

"The onions are in here. Go in and fill your bag," he said, "and be quick about it!"

Z'Onion Joe went into the bare room. It was dim inside and contained only a musty-smelling, lumpy mattress lying on a rickety iron bedstead. The old man looked around in the near darkness, but not one onion could he find. "I do not see any *z'onions* in here," he began, "but there is *beaucoup* in the root cellar. I will go fill my bag there."

But before Z'Onion Joe could turn around and see what was happening, the farmer quickly slammed the heavy door. The old man tried the door, but it was locked. "Why do you lock me in?" he demanded. "What harm have I done you?"

"You have cheated us!" yelled the farmer. "We know your secret! We know there is treasure in those onions, and we mean to have it. Teach us your magic spell, and hand over that *gris-gris* knife. We want to live forever too. Give us what we want or you will die!"

"But I have no charm, no spell. I will not live forever," cried Z'Onion Joe. "My days are numbered in this life. There is no treasure in my onions—only the gift of sweet flavor. You gotta let me go! I tell you there is no charm. I don't know any spell!"

The woman only laughed bitterly. "You cannot trick us, old man," she snarled, "we are too smart for your lies. You will tell us your secrets soon enough, when your belly screams for food and your dry throat aches for a sip of cool water!"

The farmer and his wife stomped away, hooting at the cleverness of their plan. Now they would get what they wanted. Once they took possession of the spell and the charmed knife, then they would be as happy as Z'Onion Joe.

The old man tried his strength against the door, but it

was no use. The door was too heavy and the lock too strong for him to break down. He sat in the room day after day waiting. By the third day his throat was a parched desert. His body was wracked with hunger, and his eyes dimmed until he saw things that weren't there. Everywhere juicy, sweet onions floated around his head, but when he reached to grab one, it only disappeared. For nearly a hundred years Z'Onion Joe had lived a peaceful life in the wild swamp, savoring the simple pleasures of life. Now the old man grew weaker and weaker. Z'Onion Joe knew the ragged mattress he lay upon would soon be his deathbed.

On the evening of the third day, he heard the rattle of a key turning in the lock. Slowly the door creaked open. Seeing the old man's weakened condition, the farmer and his wife swaggered into the room and began to taunt Z'Onion Joe.

"Old man," purred the farmer's wife, "look what I have brought you. Cool, fresh water, and onions, baked, boiled, and fried. Can't you just taste them? Wouldn't you like a taste of your sweet, beloved onions?"

Z'Onion Joe weakly lifted his head. "*Donne-moi des z'onions,*" he whispered. "Give me my *z'onions.*"

The woman made as if she would give the poor man a taste of an onion, then quickly snatched it away. "All you have to do is tell us the spell!" she hissed. "Teach us how to make the *gris-gris* with your knife!"

Z'Onion Joe shook his head and moaned, "There is no spell, no charm."

"Tell us the secret!" the farmer threatened, "or we'll

let you die! Why should you be the only one to cheat death with your magic and live forever? I tell you, give us what we want or we'll keep all these onions for ourselves. We'll take your charmed knife. Then you can't make your *gris-gris* and you will surely die!"

"There is no secret, no *gris-gris*. Please," Z'Onion Joe pleaded, "*donne-moi des z'onions!*"

"No!" shouted the farmer, "We're gonna keep'em all for ourselves unless you tell us the secret of eternal life. We know it's in them onions and that knife! I want that spell, and I want it NOW!"

A strange light suddenly came into the old man's eyes. With his last bit of strength, Z'Onion Joe raised himself up in bed and begged hoarsely, "Me, I'm gonna ask ya'll one more time. DONNE-MOI DES Z'ONIONS!"

"NO! We're gonna keep all these onions for ourselves!" the woman cried.

"My wife is right," sneered the farmer. "If you won't tell us the secret, then you die!"

"All right then," whispered Z'Onion Joe, his eyes blazing. "If it's a spell you want, then a spell you will have. I am only a poor man soon to leave this life. Me, I have no power to make a spell. But *Le Bon Dieu* has the might to avenge my death. He will punish you. I call upon Him to set a curse on you."

The ancient man pointed a bony, trembling finger at his captors. "After this time, you will always be reminded of your greed. When you cut into *z'onions* the air is gonna fill with the foul smell of your own rotten, stinkin', greedy hearts. Your eyes will sting and burn like fire. You'll weep bitter tears forever in memory of Z'Onion Joe who you killed outta your selfish greed!"

With that, Z'Onion Joe spat three times, and with one last satisfied sigh, he fell back dead. The farmer buried him in a shallow grave that was soon overgrown with honeysuckle vine and wild onions. The wife found the old man's knife with his little bundle of rags that had served him as clothes. *Fool,* she thought, *you could have been rich if you had played along with us. But we will find your secret yet. Now we have the knife. Soon enough we'll discover your magic spell too.*

That night the couple fingered the knife and tried to conjure the magic out of it. But it was no use; nothing was happening.

Suddenly, the farmer slammed his hands on the table. "What we need is an onion!" he exclaimed. "Of course, that's it! That's why that ol' man had to have 'em, so he could make his spell! Wife, fetch me the biggest onion you can find!"

The woman did as her husband demanded and quickly returned with a huge onion. Holding the bulb in his hand, the man prepared to make a *gris-gris*.

"Wait," said his wife fearfully, "what about the old man's curse?"

"What of it?" he scoffed. "Z'Onion Joe ain't got no power over me. Now, shut up!"

The brute held the onion up and chanted three times the dying words of Z'Onion Joe:

"Donne-moi des z'onions, donne-moi des z'onions,
DONNE-MOI DES Z'ONIONS!"

Then he spat three times just as the old man had done and sliced the onion clear in half. As if from a distance, they could hear a low, moaning voice chanting,

"DONNE-MOI DES Z'ONIONS ... DONNE-MOI DES Z'ONIONS ... DONNE-MOI DES Z'ONIONS!"

Just then the knife crumbled into ashes and disappeared in a cloud of smoke. A heavy, pungent stench filled the room and surrounded the terrified man and woman like a putrid fog. Their eyes began to burn and they rubbed them frantically to ease the pain. Tears oozed and dripped from their red, swollen eyes without end.

From that time on, they hid themselves from the world. No one could stand to come near them; their smell was too disgusting. Their flesh began to peel away from their bones just like the skin of an onion. At last, like onions left in a forgotten corner to mold and ruin, the farmer and his wife rotted away into a slimy nothing.

To this day, the curse of Z'Onion Joe survives. Whenever we cut into an onion, an awful burning odor fills our eyes with tears. We weep for poor Z'Onion Joe, a simple, peaceful old man who was murdered out of foolish, selfish greed. And that, *padnat*, is the reason why *z'onions* make us cry.

The Singing Bones

This tale is my contemporary interpretation of a traditional Cajun story. Like the Hansel and Gretel fairy tale, this story may have evolved from real events. In the fourteenth century, the bubonic plague swept across Europe. One out of three people perished. Following on the heels of the "Black Death" came a great famine. It is documented that some people, driven mad by starvation, consumed human flesh. This story may have grown up as a strong warning to those who break the taboos of society. The tale may also have offered children hope for justice and righteousness.

There was once a widower who had twenty-five children. For true, he had so many children that he lost count of them. Their poor mama had died, and the family couldn't get along without her. Papa couldn't work and care for the children too, so he looked for a new wife. But the only woman who would have him was an ugly ol' thing with a sharp tongue and a heart cold as stone. He married her anyway. After all, a poor man with so many children can't be too choosy. The children soon found their *belle-mère* to be cruel. Little by little she took the money her husband gave her for food and secretly buried it under a big rock.

The children began to complain of hunger, for she only gave them a little rice each day. Belle-Mère whipped the children hard for their complaints, and they soon learned to suffer in silence. Papa came home after the children were asleep. He ate his good supper never knowing that his children went hungry. It wasn't long before Belle-Mère begrudged the children even the little food she had been giving them. She began to think of some way that she could take even more money for herself.

My husband is so blind, she thought, *he doesn't even know how many children he has! There must surely be a way I can keep him fed and hide away more money for myself. When I have a nice nest egg laid by, I'll leave him and his whinin' brats. Then it'll be too late for him to do anything to stop me.*

Now, one day Papa came home as usual, hungry and too tired to take much notice of his wife or ask after his children. Belle-Mère served him his supper of rice, beans, and meat with no bones. It seemed to him the meat had an unusual taste.

"How is it that this meat has no bones?" he asked.

"Bones are heavy; meat is cheaper without bones," the woman snapped.

Papa ate quietly for a while. "Why is it you only eat the rice and beans?" he asked.

"I have no teeth. How can you expect me to chew meat without teeth?"

"That is true," he said. Papa kept quiet for fear of

making his wife angry, for she was as hot-tempered as she was ugly.

Papa seldom saw all twenty-five of his children at one time. A few would always be running here or there, so he didn't notice if a few were gone. In truth, he took little notice of his extra-large family.

One Sunday morning the house seemed quieter than usual. Thinking the children must be up to no good, he called them to him. But there were only four pairs of twins, two sets of triplets, and one toddler.

"Where are the others?" he asked Belle-Mère.

"What others?" she asked.

"It seems to me I have many more children than these," he said with a frown.

"You do not even know how many children you have, and you ask me where they are? If you care so much, they've gone to see their *grandmaman*," she retorted, "to help the poor ol' thing with her chores. They'll be back in a few weeks."

This didn't seem strange to Papa as the children often visited their *grandmaman*. He said no more about it, not caring to throw his wife into a rage.

Things went on as before. Papa left early and returned late, too tired to ask about his children. Belle-Mère served him his supper of rice, beans, and meat without bones. One night he again grew curious about the flavor of the meat.

"Wife," he asks, "what kind of meat is this? I never tasted meat like this before."

Belle-Mère flew into a rage. "First you complain there

aren't any bones, when I am only tryin' to save money. Now you're complainin' about my cookin'. Well, if you don't like it, then you can just buy the meat and cook it yourself!"

Papa was too tired to argue with Belle-Mère and her sharp tongue, so he just let the matter drop. Anyway, the meat wasn't bad-tasting, just unusual.

He ate his supper, thinking, *She's right, the house and the children are her business. Why should I be concerned with woman's work?*

The days passed, and each night Papa ate his supper of rice, beans, and meat with no bones. He didn't ask any more questions about the meat or his children. But one Sunday morning he got to thinking that the house was deathly quiet.

Now what are those children up to? he wondered. *It's way too quiet.* "Come children," he called, "come to your papa!"

One by one the children began to appear, as though they had been hiding in the cracks. Papa soon saw something was wrong, though. There was only one set of twins and the youngest child.

"Where are your brothers and sisters?" he asked.

The children looked at their stepmother with frightened eyes and said nothing.

"Old man," snaps Belle-Mère, "are you complaining again? The children are visiting their *grandmaman*, of course. They will be back in a few weeks. Now hush and stop botherin' us with questions!"

After supper, Papa sat out on a big rock under a great live oak tree, enjoying his evening rest. He watched his three children playing quietly under the tree. They seemed so sad and so thin. He began to think of his other children and how he missed their games and laughter. He was on the point of going to get them from their *grandmaman* when suddenly he heard his missing children singing sweetly. Their voices seemed to come from far away.

The children are on their way back home, he thought happily.

The singing grew louder until he could make out the words of their song:

> *Our stepmother killed us,*
> *Our papa ate us,*
> *We are not in a coffin,*
> *We are not in the cemetery,*
> *Holy, holy, holy.*

Papa thought his ears were failing him. "What kind of song is this?" he called out. "Come to Papa, my little ones. Tell me why you sing such a strange song!"

The sweet voices started singing again, closer and louder than before:

> *Our stepmother killed us,*
> *Our papa ate us,*
> *We are not in a coffin,*
> *We are not in the cemetery,*
> *Holy, holy, holy.*

The singing seemed to surround Papa, to flow from the very stone he sat upon. He got down on his knees and put his ear to the rock. Once again he heard his children singing, sweet as angels:

> *Our stepmother killed us,*
> *Our papa ate us,*
> *We are not in a coffin,*
> *We are not in the cemetery,*
> *Holy, holy, holy.*

With trembling hands, Papa rolled the stone away. To his horror, there lay a great mound of small human bones, half-buried in the earth. The bones began to sing:

> *Our stepmother killed us,*
> *Our papa ate us,*
> *We are not in a coffin,*
> *We are not in the cemetery,*
> *Holy, holy, holy.*

Bitter tears fell from Papa's eyes, and his heart broke as he realized the truth: his cruel wife had killed the children and cooked them, and he had eaten them, his own flesh and blood! He fell on his knees, crying, "Ah, my children, forgive me! Why didn't I ask about you? Why didn't I watch out for you like a good father? I should have seen what was happenin'."

Papa leaped to his feet with murder in his heart. "Belle-Mère," he screamed, "you're gonna pay for my children's lives!"

He ran up to the house, but he was too late. When Belle-Mère heard the singing and knew that she had been discovered, she slipped out by the back door and ran down to the rock where her money was buried. She meant to dig it up and escape. She clawed through the dirt around the the children's bones, frantic for her money.

Suddenly, the bones began to sing, louder and louder like the wailing wind of a storm, until the ground rumbled and split. The sky opened up and heaven's fury broke loose upon her. A mighty lightning bolt struck Belle-Mère right between her eyes with a booming crack! The wicked woman exploded into a heap of dust.

Gradually the storm beat itself out. A warm rain began to fall, like teardrops from heaven, washing away the dust until the children's bones were white as snow and no trace remained of Belle-Mère.

Papa put his children's bones in a coffin and buried it in the cemetery beside the grave of their true mother. For the rest of his life he never again touched meat, haunted by the meat that had no bones. He lived in great sorrow for his murdered children, and his heart was heavy with his own guilt. He wished to be released from his burden, and he prayed for death, but heaven punished him instead with a very long life.

Madame Longfingers

Generations of Cajun children have grown up with many different stories of Madame Longfingers, also known as Madame Grand Doights. Whether told for entertainment or as a warning to naughty children, the story of this bony-fingered, toe-snatchin' witch has scared many children into nightmares. As a child with a vivid imagination, I was certain the witch lived under my bed. Here is my original story, dedicated to all those children who have ever slept with their toes tucked up under their chins!

L ittle Rufus was the apple of his Mama's eye, at least until the day he took his first step. From that point on it was downhill all the way, straight into trouble. It wasn't that he was a mean-spirited boy; he was just curious as a cat. Rufus couldn't help himself. He was chock full of whys, and how-comes and what-ifs. Where some children are good at singing or spelling or such, Rufus had a talent for stirring up trouble. He attracted calamity like a magnet; disaster was his middle name.

By the time he was seven, Rufus was a legend across the parish. He fell down the well trying to find out if it really was as cold as he'd heard; brought home a baby cottonmouth snake to be his playmate; broke his arm and nearly his neck trying to fly out of a giant live oak tree; cut the whiskers off the cat; rode the cow swayback; and set the house on fire trying to send Indian smoke signals out the chimney.

His papa and mama tried everything they knew to keep their boy out of mischief, but nothing worked. They watched him like a hawk, but the minute their back was turned Rufus was out the door, up a tree, or down the bayou. Of course, they got plenty of child-raising advice from other folks. It seemed like everybody thought they knew how to cure Rufus of getting into so much trouble.

"Worms," said the old ladies, "That's the boy's problem, worms. Feed 'im cayenne pepper and garlic, that'll settle him down."

"He's moon sick," declared the old men. "Must be sleepin' in the moonlight. Everybody knows the moon'll make your eyes go crossed and get you nervy as a gnat."

One day, round, wrinkly, Aunt Noo Noo came to visit. She eyed Rufus up quick-quick. "Worms? Phooey!" exclaimed the old lady. "Moon-sick, my foot. The boy's problem is that he does not know fear. Rufus hasn't learned that curiosity killed the cat! Give him to me for awhile. I'll fix him all right."

Mama and Papa listened carefully. After all, Tante Noo Noo had special healing powers. She could cure warts better than any other *traiteur* in the parish. If anybody could get Rufus to settle down, it was Tante Noo Noo. Mama and Papa decided to send Rufus to the old woman's *cabane*.

She would teach the boy about fear, then maybe he would not be so curious.

Rufus wasn't too sure he wanted to go visit Tante Noo Noo. Her cabin was dark and shadowy and smelled like old snuff jars and talcum powder. The old woman was a pincher too. She'd grab on to Rufus's rosy cheeks and hang on like a crawfish snatching a piece of bacon on a string.

"Now Rufus," said Mama with a worried smile, "you go on with Tante Noo Noo. She's gonna take good care of you. Mind her and don't be a sassyfras."

Rufus drove away with Tante Noo Noo in her dead husband's old wagon, pulled by an ancient, lop-eared mule called Bill. They rode for what seemed like an eternity to the little boy, who was trying really hard to be good. He was itching to wiggle his bare toes in the mud along the bayou bank or poke his nose down a dark hole to see what kind of beady-eyed thing he could find. All of a sudden, his wandering fingers remembered the sling shot in the bib of his overalls. He had a nice heavy piece of shot too—a green pecan with a little, sharp-pointed end.

Hmmm, Rufus thought. *Wonder what would happen if I gave ol' Bill a little shot of pick-up? Why, I bet he'd get us back quick for true! I'd just be helpin' Tante Noo Noo. I 'magine she'll gimme a big bowl of rice puddin' for helpin' her get on back home.*

Rufus got out his slingshot. He had carved it himself with his very own jackknife and strung it with a strip of an old Model T tire tube. It was his pride and joy. He glanced over at Tante Noo Noo. The poor ol' thing was dozing while the mule plodded slow as molasses down the familiar dirt path. The boy set his pecan in the rubber sling, stretched it tight, took aim at the mule's swaying rump, and SHOOM! He let go of that sling and the pecan whizzed through the air like a green dart, striking Bill square on his right haunch.

The mule brayed and took off like a bolt of lightning down the rutted path. Tante Noo Noo waked with a jerk to find her *garde-soleil* pulled over her eyes and her false choppers rattling in her mouth.

"Whoa, boy, whoa!" she hollered, pulling back on the reins. But it was no use. The reins had got loose from her hands. Blindfolded as she was, she couldn't see she was pulling on her own bonnet strings. The wagon was bumping like a square wheel. Rufus was hanging on to his straw hat, whooping it up. He was having the ride of his life. They were headed for Bayou Chinquapin when the wagon struck a deep rut. It jolted so hard that it sent the boy and the old woman flying through the air. Rufus and Tante Noo Noo splashed into the bayou, and the mule and wagon came plunging in after them. The mule and the woman were mad as a nest of stirred-up hornets.

Tante Noo Noo pulled herself slipping and sliding out of the bayou while Rufus watched from the bank and wiggled his toes in the mud. Finally she stood dripping, hands on her wide hips, glaring down at the boy.

"Rufus," she said, "do you have any idea why that mule went crazy?"

"Well," he said thoughtfully, "It just mighta been that

pecan that hit 'im."

"What pecan?"

"Oh, the one I shot him with, outta my slingshot," said Rufus with big eyes. "I just wanted to see what would happen. Oowhee, he sure did get a move on!"

"Rufus, you are the baddest boy that ever lived on the bayou! *Cher*, didn't you know you were gonna scare that mule and me nearly to death?" she asked. "What is the matter for you? You didn't even have sense to be scared yourself. Why, I don't believe you are scared of nothin'! You better watch out, you are just the kind of ugly little boy that Madame Longfingers comes lookin' for in the night!"

"Who," asked Rufus, "is Madame Longfingers?"

"I tell you what, Rufus," said Tante Noo Noo with a little crooked smile, "let's go catch that crazy mule and get on home. After supper I'll tell you all about Madame Longfingers."

That night Rufus tried hard to be good. He cleaned up two big bowls of gumbo and let Aunt Noo Noo scrub his neck and behind his ears. The old woman fixed him a pallet of quilts on the floor before the hearth. A little fire burned to take the chill off the night. Tante Noo Noo sat in her rocking chair and looked down at the boy.

"Now, Rufus," she said, "I am gonna tell you all about Madame Longfingers. But I gotta warn you, boy, do not scoff at her, *mais non!* She's a bad one, and she'll come lookin' for you on some dark night. Just the sight of her is enough to freeze your blood!"

"What does she look like?" Rufus asked eagerly.

"Madame Longfingers is the ugliest thing that ever lived," Tante Noo Noo said in a hushed voice. "She's got an ol' scaly lizard-green face with red, burning eyes, and jaggedy rotten yellow teeth. Her nose is long and sharp, with a great big wart growin' on the tip. Her hair is tangly as a thicket, and she's so skinny she's nothin' but a skin and bones. But worst of all, she has got fingers that are so long and knotted and bony they look just like ol' twisty tree roots. That Madame Longfingers is always lookin' for plump, little child toes to yank in the middle of the night.

"Oohwhee," said Rufus, grinning ear to ear. "I'd like to see that ol' witch for true!"

"Hush your mouth, boy!" she scolded. "You never know when she is creepin' around, just lookin' for a bad child to get her hands on. She'll wait till you are fast asleep, then she'll come creepin' in soft as a shadow through the window. First, she likes to give your quilt a little tug, like a cat playing with a mouse. Then, Madame Longfingers takes her long-long, bony fingers and grabs your big toe. She'll pull and pull until she snatches your toe clean off your foot!"

Rufus's eyes were about to pop out of his head, he was so excited. "How come she wants toes?" he asked in a loud whisper. "What does she do with 'em?"

"Nobody knows, Rufus. There just no tellin' what awful thing she does with all those toes she's yanked off bad children's feet."

"Tante Noo Noo, do you think she might come pull my toes?" the boy asked hopefully. "I was awful bad today, don't ya think so?"

The old woman sighed heavily and shook her head. "Rufus, have you got moss between your ears? You don't want that ol' witch comin' around. You oughta be scared and be a good boy so she'll stay away! Why in the world would you want Madame Longfingers to come pull your toes?"

"Aw, I'm just curious, that's all. Maybe I could build a witch trap," he said. "Made me a gator trap one time, caught one too, only Mama made me put it back."

"Well, curiosity killed the cat," the old woman snapped crankily. "It would just serve you right if that witch snatched all your toes off for bein' such a sassy, nosy little boy. A good scare is just what you need to straighten you out! Now, me, I'm goin' to bed. Don't you be wakin' me up in the night if ol' Longfingers comes to getcha."

The old woman headed off to her bed, leaving Rufus alone on his pallet watching the flickering shadows on the walls. The boy thought and thought about Madame Longfingers. *Well,* he said to himself, *I'm not scared even if I was plenty bad today. If that ol' witch comes, she's in for a big surprise, mais oui, 'cause me, I'm gonna set a trap for her.*

Rufus jumped out of bed and pulled on his overalls. He went over to the cookstove and fished a tasty shrimp out of the gumbo pot. He grabbed a sack, some string, and stuffed a pair of pliers into his pocket. The boy climbed out the window into the moonlit night. In no time at all he found some crawfish hills. He tied the shrimp to the string and dropped it down a hole. There was a little tug, and Rufus pulled up a big crawfish. He kept on crawfishing till he had a dozen good-sized crawfish in his sack. He picked an armload of moss and headed back to the *cabane.*

Rufus stuffed the moss under his quilt to make it look like a sleeping boy. Then he emptied his bag of angry, pinching crawfish at the foot of his bed and covered them up with the quilt. *That ought to fix her,* he thought. *When that witch reaches in to pull my toes, she'll be sorry for true. Those crawfish are gonna pinch her bony fingers black and blue!*

The boy crept into a dark, shadowy corner to wait for Madame Longfingers. Soon after he drifted off to sleep, he waked to the sound of someone creeping across the room and then crouching down low by the moss-stuffed pallet. The figure turned toward the fire for a moment, and Rufus saw that it was Madame Longfingers! Tante Noo Noo was right. She was the ugliest thing that ever lived. Her green face was shriveled up, and her eyes burned like fiery coals. Her hair was a rat's nest, and her skeleton hands had long, green, bony fingers.

Suddenly the witch looked straight at the dark corner where Rufus was hiding. Had she seen him? The boy's heart thumped so hard he thought he'd drop dead right there on the spot. But no, now she was reaching under the quilt, searching for—toes! Just then the witch let out a yowl that made Rufus's hair stand on end. When she pulled out her knotty hands, he saw there was a crawfish hanging onto every horrible bony finger. Those crawfish were pinching the daylights out of her as she tried to shake them off. Quick as a cat, Madame Longfingers leaped through the window, waving her bony fingers and howling to wake the dead.

Just as quick, Rufus jumped through the window. That witch had nearly scared him to death, but now he was just about to die of curiosity to see what would happen next. He followed Madame Longfingers quiet as a moonbeam down the bayou. At last he saw her climb up into a giant live oak tree. So that was where she lived, in a tree house. The boy waited and waited till the witch quit hollering, and he counted ten crawfish tossed out her window.

Rufus climbed the tree silently. A question was just itching in his head. *What does she do with all those toes she's plucked off of bad children?* He climbed through the window of the tree house. There was Madame Longfingers, asleep in her bed, snoring loudly in the moonlight. Rufus tip-toed over and raised the bedcover ever so lightly. There were the witch's long, green, bony toes pointing at the roof. With a big grin, he took the pliers out of his overalls. *All right you bag of bones*, he thought, *now you gonna get a taste of your own medicine.* Rufus opened the pliers and grabbed the hag's big toe. He pinched as hard as he could and held on for dear life.

Madame Longfingers waked screeching, "Yeeow! Who's got my toe? Let go of my toe!" She fixed her burning glare on the little boy at the foot of the bed. "So," she hissed, "It's you. I mighta known. Yow! Quit that pinchin', let go of my long, green, bony big toe!"

But Rufus just pinched harder. "Yeeoow!" she hollered. "You bad, ugly boy, let go of my long, green, bony, big toe!"

"You gotta promise to leave me alone, then I'll let go of your toe."

"Ha! Nothin' doin' you nosy, sassy brat! You deserve to get your toes pulled!" the witch hissed.

"Well then," the boy exclaimed, "if you won't promise, then I'll pull and pull until ..." All of a sudden, there was a big POP. Rufus looked down at the pliers in his hand. He had pulled off the witch's long, green, bony big toe!

"Aaiiee, my toe! Gimme back my long, green, bony big toe!"

"Now do you promise to leave me alone?"

"I promise, I PROMISE. Just gimme back my long, green, bony big toe!"

"And there's one more thing," Rufus said. "Tell me what you do with bad children's toes."

"Oh, all right then," she whined. "If you gotta know, I go fishin' with 'em. I'm so ugly, why, I can't even get close to the water. Those fish see me, and they just run and hide in the *boscoyo*. Well, even an ol' witch has got to eat! So I have to trick the fish. I just rub my bait good with some of that brat's toe. Those fish just love the flavor so, they'll sneak out and swallow my bait. Now that you know what I do with those stinky, nasty little brat toes," she hissed, GIMME BACK MY LONG, GREEN, BONY BIG TOE!"

Suddenly Rufus had an idea. *I wonder ...*, he thought,

and he snapped off a piece of the witch's toe and hid it in his pocket. "Here's your ol' ugly toe," he said, tossing it across the room.

While she scrambled to catch her big toe, the boy climbed out of the tree house and dropped to the ground. As he ran away he could hear Madame Longfingers hollering after him.

"MY TOE, WHAT DID YOU DO TO MY LONG, GREEN, BONY BIG TOE?" Sure enough, when the witch stuck it back on her foot, she saw her toe was only half as long. "OHHHH," she cried, "What am I gonna do with a SHORT, GREEN, BONY BIG TOE?"

Rufus ran back and crawled through the window and lay down on his pallet. Tante Noo Noo was in the back of the *cabane* snoring like a buzzsaw. *Well,* he told himself, *she said not to wake her up if Madame Longfingers came to get me. I'll tell her all about it in the mornin'.*

The next day Rufus told Tante Noo Noo about his adventure with Madame Longfingers. He wasn't quite sure she believed him, not even when he showed her the chunk of witch's toe, which now looked a lot like a piece of withered root. Well, grown-ups were like that sometimes. When Tante Noo Noo asked him if he got scared, she seemed satisfied when he told her, *mais oui*, he was scared for true, at least for a little while.

"Good, Rufus," she said, "I see that my little story did you some good. Now that you know what fear is, maybe you'll be a nice boy and stay out of trouble."

Rufus did mostly stay out of trouble after that. He was

way too busy fishing, pulling in whoppers, one after the other. By the time he was twelve, he was a legend among fisherman. "How do you it, Rufus?" the old men asked enviously. The old ladies tried to bribe the boy with pecan pies and fig cakes to find out the source of his luck, but Rufus kept quiet. He knew he had discovered the fishing secret of the ages.

One little rub of that witch's toe on his bait and SHOOM! Fish leap right out of the water to snatch it, 'cause if there's one thing in this world that fish like better than a bad little brat's toes, it's a witch's long, green, bony big toe.

The Nightmare Witch

Many people have felt overwhelmed in their sleep by a frightening force which they can only name as a terrible nightmare. The Cajun people personalized this terror as the cauchemar, *a witch that particularly fell upon young people who were beginning to stray from the moral path. The* cauchemar *was said to be an actual being that "rode" its victim like a horse, sometimes leaving whip marks behind as evidence of its visit. Whether a real being or a monster rising from the depths of our minds, an encounter with the* cauchemar *is a genuinely terrifying experience.*

Lucille lay on her bed daydreaming while the Saturday Night Hit Parade blared from the transistor radio she held to her ear. The DJ was just about to play the new Elvis single when she heard her mother coming up the stairs.

"Lucille, didn't you hear me callin' you?" Her mother, Blanche, stood in the doorway with her hands on her hips. "Turn off that music and go to sleep. Girl, you play that little radio loud enough to wake the dead for true. You better watch out," she teased, "that loud rock and roll music might just wake up some ol' *cauchemar*. It'll think you're a bad child keepin' everybody awake. Some dark night it'll come creepin' up with those red eyes shinin' out

from under that black pointy hat. Just as you're dreamin' of Elvis Presley, that bogeyman will give you a big bad nightmare."

Lucille rolled her eyes and spoke harshly to her mother, something she was beginning to do all too often these days. "Oh sure, a *cauchemar*," she said scornfully. "You mean the nightmare witch *Grandmaman* used to tell me about when I was little? She nearly scared me to death with those stories. She had me believin' the *cauchemar* was real, but in case you haven't noticed, I'm not a baby anymore. I'm not scared by those ol' superstitions."

"You know your *grandmaman* really believed in the *cauchemar?* That's why she used to sprinkle her pillow with Holy Water every night," Blanche said. "Father Daigle used to kid her about usin' so much Holy Water. He asked her one time if she took baths in it. She got tickled at that. "You know," Blanche said quietly, "for all her superstitions, your *grandmaman* was a wise woman in her own way. But now, *cauchemar* or not, it's time to turn off the radio and get some sleep. I don't want that music wakin' up your brothers or the baby."

Lucille ignored Blanche. Rock and roll blared between daughter and mother.

"Lucille, I said to turn that thing off now!"

"Oh, Ma," Lucille moaned dramatically. "OK,OK, it's off."

"*Bon soir, chère,*" Blanche said to her daughter, "sweet dreams."

The girl switched off her light and turned her back to

her mother, mumbling, "G'night." When her mother's steps had faded down the stairs, she clicked the radio back on, keeping the volume down low. Lucille moved the dial slowly, tuning in signals from near and far. A touch of the dial and Roy Acuff was singing "The Wabash Cannonball" on the Grand Ole Opry up in Nashville. Further down the dial she picked up "The Louisiana Hayride," and through the radio static, the distant horns of a mariachi band all the way from Mexico.

She heard a Brill Creme commercial next and was searching the dial for her favorite New Orleans station when a deep radio voice thundered in her ear: "And soooo, Ol' Devil, I say—y, to you—u and all your kind, LOOK OU—T! 'Cause we got us a whole flock of prayer warriors here tonight. And now, the Jubilee Sisters are gonna sing your favorite and mine, "Turn Your Radio On ..."

Lucille quickly clicked the radio off. *Brother Duke sure is preachin' up a storm tonight on the All-Night Gospel Show,* she thought. *That local station comes in loud and clear for true. Sounded like he was preachin' right here in the room. Good thing Mama didn't hear. Well, I might as well go to sleep anyway. Don't want the batteries to get low.* Lucille hugged her pillow and fell asleep with the radio still in her hand.

The house was quiet and dark when a sudden cold draft of air made her shiver. From the middle of a dream she reached for her quilt. Something tugged it back.

"Mama ... that you," she mumbled, pulling the warm cover up a second time. She had drifted off again when the quilt slid off the bed. Still half-asleep, Lucille groggily opened her eyes a crack, and her heart suddenly pounded with an electric jolt.

To her horror, she saw the silhouette of a tall figure standing at the foot of her bed. Two red eyes burned like coals in the shadows of the hooded cloak that draped its bony shape. The girl froze with fear, only a small gasp escaping her lips. It was the nightmare witch!

In an instant the thing was upon her neck, choking her and prodding her in the ribs with it's bony claws. She struggled to cry out for help, but she was powerless against her dreadful attacker. Her terrified mind raced with thoughts of her grandmother and Holy Water. She could not utter a word nor lift a muscle, so great was the *cauchemar's* spell.

She felt herself rising up against her will. The thing was taking her to the open window. She knew it meant to fling her down to the ground below. With all of her strength, Lucille fought to free herself from the deadly nightmare witch.

Downstairs, Lucille's mother was sleeping peacefully when she was startled out of her sleep. "Blanche," said a voice, "Blanche, wake up." She sat up in bed, rubbing her eyes. *I must have been dreaming of Mama,* she thought. *That was her voice, I'd know it anywhere. Now, why would I dream of her telling me to wake-up?* Blanche laid back down, wishing her husband was home from his overnight fishing trip.

She lay quietly for a moment, until at last she rose to

check on the baby. *Sleepin' fine*, she thought. Peeking into the boys' room, she saw that they were also sound asleep in their usual tangled heap of sheets and bed toys. She paused at the foot of the stairs. *What a silly I am*, she thought, *running around the house in the middle of the night just 'cause I had a strange dream.* She started off to bed but turned back and quietly tip-toed up the stairs. *Maybe Lucille is nearly grown-up, but she is still my little girl.*

Blanche stepped lightly onto the upstairs landing and quietly opened the door of her daughter's room. Her hair stood on end when she saw Lucille, standing on the window ledge. The girl's arms were flailing wildly and her face was a mask of raw terror.

"Lucille," Blanche called softly to her daughter. "It's Mama, honey." Her heart pounding, Blanche grasped her daughter's clawing hands. "Wake up, Lucille, you're dreamin'. C'mon, honey, it's all right. Mama's here." The girl fought her mother like a wildcat and then fell limp and exhausted into her arms.

She waked trembling in an icy sweat. "Oh, Mama," she gasped, "it was the nightmare witch, the *cauchemar*. It tried to throw me from the window!"

"Shh. It's all right now," Blanche said gently. "You were dreamin' baby. Go on back to sleep. It was only a nightmare."

"No, Mama, it wasn't a dream. It was real," Lucille said in a frightened whisper. "It was just like the stories Grandmaman told me. I tried so hard to fight it, but I couldn't even say a prayer like she taught me, to scare it away."

"Well, I should not have been teasin' you about the *cauchemar*," Blanche said, "that's what made you dream of it. Now, you lay down and go to sleep ..." She looked into her daughter's frightened eyes and thought of her own strange dream. "You go to sleep and I'm gonna sit here in this rocking chair. I'll stay right by you, *chère*, OK?"

The girl lay back on her pillow and shut her eyes. Blanche sat in the chair and rocked slowly until she heard Lucille breathing slow and easy. Satisfied her daughter was asleep, she rested her head on a cushion and soon drifted off into her own dreams.

It was an hour before dawn when Lucille sensed an evil presence in the room. Like a diver rising from a great depth, she struggled to wake herself from a deep slumber. She tried to call her mother, but as she spoke she realized it was too late. No sound came from her lips. The spell of the *cauchemar* was already upon her.

As it seized her throat with its bony claws, Lucille fought to clear her mind. Now it was pulling her up again to the window. She desperately tried to think of some way to escape the *cauchemar's* iron grip. Suddenly she became aware of something in her hand, a hard box—no wait, it was her radio. "Turn ... the radio ... on," said a clear, calm voice in her head. From some unknown source of strength within her, she willed her finger to move the dial.

Instantly the radio came to life as the sound of Brother Duke's All-Night Gospel Show filled the room. "My friends-s, a devil is a devil-l, no matter what name it goes by—y. Sooo, I say—y, in the name of Heaven—n, DEVIL—L, GET UP AND GET OUT!"

At that moment Lucille felt the weight of the *cauchemar* fly from her. She was free. The nightmare witch was gone! She bolted up wide awake, laughing with joy. Blanche sat up suddenly and switched on the light. She was pale and trembling. "Are you all right?" she demanded.

"I'm fine now, Mama," Lucille said, catching her breath. "You were sleeping when the *cauchemar* came back again. I was trying so hard to wake you, but I couldn't make a sound. Then I heard a voice in my head telling me to turn the radio on." The girl saw a strange expression on her mother's face. "What is it, Mama?" she asked. "Why are you lookin' at me so funny?"

"Tonight I heard a voice in my dream too," Blanche said slowly. The voice told me to wake up. I thought it was your *grandmaman* speaking to me. That's when I got up to check on all you kids and found you fixin' to go out the window!"

Mother and daughter looked at each other in silence for a long time, each knowing the other's thoughts.

"Well, girl," Blanche said at last, "what a night this has been. Whatever or whoever made you turn that radio on, I sure am glad you did. What a dream I was havin'! Two big ol' red shinin' eyes were comin' after me … thank goodness for that radio."

"You know, Mama," Lucille said thoughtfully, "it

must have been Brother Duke's preachin' that scared off that nightmare witch."

"Well," Blanche said, "I always did think Brother Duke was a little scary myself!"

Together they laughed hard with relief until Blanche stood up and headed for the stairs.

"Goin' to bed, Mama?" Lucille asked. "It's OK. I'm not scared of any ol' *cauchemar*. Now I know how to fix that nightmare witch good."

"Goin' back to bed," Blanche said, "are you kiddin'? Me, I'm not takin' anymore chances with nightmare witches, *mais non*! I'm goin' downstairs to get you some more batteries for that wonderful little transistor radio of yours. And as soon as it's light, I'm gonna call up Father Daigle and order us about a gallon of Holy Water!"

A Promise Is a Promise

This tale is based on a true account I heard from a neighbor in Thibodaux, Louisiana. I have collected many curious stories over the years just as I have had my own unexplainable experiences. Once, during an emergency with my child, I somehow communicated with my husband who was miles away. When he "heard" my plea and "saw" a mental image of our injured toddler, he quickly hurried home. Coincidence or supernatural happening? I may never know. Perhaps the real truth in this kind of story is in its testimony to the incredible power of love.

Inez Guillory sat in a metal lawnchair on the shaded *galerie* of her next-door neighbor and best friend, Yvonne Dubois. Out in the yard, a colorful line of wash danced on the summer breeze. Roses rambled delicately up a white fan trellis which leaned lazily against the railing. The flowers' fragrance wafted up to the porch where the two old women often gathered after their morning chores to enjoy a cup of steaming chicory coffee and a few tidbits of juicy gossip.

These days they lingered over their coffee, unlike the early years of their friendship. Back then, their days had been filled with cooking, cleaning, husbands and lots of noisy children. Their daily visit was an excuse for the two weary young mothers to rest for a spell and catch up on all the news. For fifty years they had been meeting nearly every day at one house or the other, and a friendship had grown between them that was as sweet and strong as the coffee they sipped from cracked china cups.

Mostly they talked about the goings-on around them—about children and grandchildren, recipes, weather, church news, and old men. But on this warm June day their talk was full of memories of all the joys and sorrows they had shared through the years.

"You know, *chère*," said Yvonne, "I can't think what I would've done without you. We've been through some trouble for true. I was just now thinkin' about that time when my Little Joe was so sick with fever and how you watched all my *bébés* for three days. You got some gray hair from that, *mais oui*, cooped up with your six and my other four, and it rainin' the whole time!"

Inez laughed and took a sip of her coffee. "You're right about that," she agreed. "But you have been like a sister to me, better than a sister. Hey, remember how my Yvette got stuck way up in that tree? She was just clinging up there like a cat for dear life. I just knew she was gonna fall and break her little neck. There I was, big as a barn, expectin' Leo and couldn't do a thing, but you jumped up that tree and carried that child down on your own back!"

The women laughed and grew quiet. "Inez," Yvonne said, rubbing her knotted arthritic hands, "I just thought that maybe I should tell you what a good friend you have been to me. After all, we're not getting any younger. Here lately, well, I haven't been feelin' too good ..."

"Now hush that kind of talkin'," Inez said sternly. "Didn't that new doctor tell you just last week you were doin' fine? Oh, I know you can't see so good anymore, but nobody ever passed on from bad eyesight, eh? You can still make the best gumbo around, I guarantee."

Yvonne smiled a little. "Oh, I get by fine for true. It's ... somethin' else. It's the strangest thing. You are gonna think I've lost what little sense I ever had when I tell you. Here lately, I have been hearin' my Joe, just clear as a bell. And you know what, it didn't scare me at all. It was just as natural as daylight. I tell you the truth, I hear him call my name and it's like I can feel him near me. Nothin' like that has happened since he passed ten years ago."

Inez listened quietly. "I don't think you're crazy," she said at last. "Of course, you gonna miss Joe. He was a good husband for forty years. I don't doubt he's watchin' over you from heaven."

Yvonne smiled. "I was thinkin'," she said softly, "maybe it's a sign. Maybe it's gonna be my time one day soon."

Inez took Yvonne's hand in her own. "That's not for us to know or worry about. Besides," she said teasing her friend, "you best not be goin' anywhere without comin' around and tellin' your best friend goodbye. I'd be downright mad at you!"

Yvonne nodded her head. "That's it," she said thoughtfully. "Let's make a promise. When our time comes, we'll do our best to say good-bye before we go."

"*Chère*, what are you talkin' about?" Inez joked, "Of course, I'll float by your place first to say goodbye and to get your gumbo recipe. Fifty years and you still won't tell me your secret ingredient!"

Yvonne chuckled in spite of herself. "Oh, Inez, you always could make me laugh. But for true now, let's promise. When it comes our time to pass, whoever goes first will do her best to come say good-bye." She held out her hand. "Promise?" she asked seriously.

Inez shook her friend's hand. "All right," she said, "it's a deal. I promise."

The two old women's talk brightened now even as the summer sky around them darkened. Together they quickly gathered the dry wash from the line. Inez helped her friend carry her load of wash up the porch steps. "Guess I better get goin'," she said looking up at the threatening clouds. "See you in the mornin' for coffee." Lightening flashed in the distance as she dashed to her own front porch just in time to beat the rain.

All through the night the thunder boomed and a heavy rain fell. Morning dawned fresh and dewy, with a cool breeze chasing the storm before it. When Inez, an early riser, looked out her kitchen window, she saw the misty arc of a rainbow crossing the clearing sky. Suddenly she was startled to hear someone calling her name. *Why, it's Yvonne,* she thought. *She must be feeling better. Oh, I've gotta tell her about the rainbow. Even if she can't see it, she'll want to hear about it. She always did love a rainbow.*

Inez went to her side window and saw Yvonne walking down the road. She raised her window and called out, "*Bon matin, ça va?* You lookin' good this mornin'. Feelin' better, *chère?*" Out on the road, Yvonne smiled and pointed to the rainbow. "What?" asked Inez surprised. "You can see the rainbow? Oh, that's wonderful. Isn't it the prettiest thing? I guess that new medicine is helpin' you after all! Let me get dressed and I'll see you in a little bit for coffee. All right then, bye-bye, I'll see you soon!"

Yvonne nodded and smiled. Then she waved a goodbye to her friend and walked on down the road with a light step. Inez watched her as she disappeared at the bend in the road. "She's walkin' right up to that rainbow to get a good look. Bless her heart, it's been years since she could see so well."

Inez had just changed into her housedress and a fresh apron when the phone rang. It was Joe, Yvonne's youngest boy. "Oh, Joe," she said, "your Mama must be tickled to see you … Gone? Yeah, I just saw her walkin' out on the road—she must be feelin' real good today. It's been a long time since she took a mornin' walk, and she even saw the rainbow … Joe? What's wrong? … Yvonne passed on in her sleep? But that can't be, I just saw her … I … What? Yes Joe, I'll be right over."

Inez put the phone down and steadied herself against the kitchen table. She walked slowly to the window and watched the rainbow fade away in the morning sunshine. "Oh, Yvonne, what am I gonna do without you?" she whispered. "During all those years you never let me down.

You always kept your promises. Thank you for coming to say goodbye ... one last time. Goodbye, my friend ... goodbye."

The old woman wiped her eyes with her apron. She smoothed her hair and put on her good black dress before she went down to Yvonne's. There was so much to do before the funeral. The house would be full of family and friends by the afternoon and they would want coffee, lots and lots of good, strong coffee.

The Haunted Hunters
of the Chasse-Galerie

I have met several people in my life who swear that they have heard the Chasse-Galerie. The eerie sound of these cursed hunters is said to make one's hair stand on end. One old gentleman told me the ghosts frightened his prize hunting hound so badly that the animal never hunted again. "After runnin' into them ghosts," he said sadly, "that dog whan't good for nothin'."

Pop Fontenot stretched his lean frame before the glowing warmth of the campfire. He pulled out his pocketwatch and checked the time. It was already after eleven, but the dogs were still running strong. He could hear them howling off in the distance, on the trail of raccoon or possum. He listened for the cry of his own dog. *There she is*, he thought, *there's good ol' Belle. I'd know her holler anywhere.*

Pop turned to the other two men sitting around the fire. "There's my Belle," he said proudly. "Sounds like she has treed herself a possum."

"Well, Pop, how come you're not goin' after it?" asked Shorty, swatting a mosquito from his bald head. "If you don't want it, maybe I'll call Ol' Hip and get that possum myself. There's nothin' like barbecued possum—whew, man, that is some good eatin', I gua-ran-tee."

"Oh, I don't know about that," Junior said, sitting up and scratching his ample, hairy belly. "Me, I don't want no possum. I'd eat armadillo before I'd eat possum. I don't mean to bad mouth Belle or Ol' Hip, but my hound Bullet wouldn't even waste his time on possum. He's picky all right, but when he howls, you know you got yourself some good eatin' game for true."

Pop shot a thin stream of tobacco juice into the fire. "Naw, boys, I'm not goin' out," he said, ignoring Junior's boast. "It's a quarter past now, time to get the dogs in. I gotta get some sleep. I'm goin' to early Mass in the mornin'. Besides, I never hunt on Sunday, and accordin' to my watch, Sunday mornin' is less than an hour away. I sure don't want to tangle with those haunted hunters of the Chasse-Galerie, *mais non.*"

"Yeah," Shorty agreed, "It's gettin' late. Me, I don't want to mess with no ghosts."

"Wait just a cotton-pickin' minute," said Junior. "Do ya'll mean to say ya'll believe all that ghost stuff? Ya'll are gonna quit, just when the dogs are goin' strong? Just 'cause ya'll believe some silly ghost story?"

"Let me tell you somethin', Junior," Pop said quietly. "If you had ever heard those hunters flyin' in the night like me, you would not be so sure the Chasse-Galerie is just a story."

Junior cracked up with laughter. His belly shook like

jelly beneath his tight T-shirt. "Whoa, *mon padnat*," he said, between guffaws. "Man, this I gotta hear. C'mon, Pop, out with it."

The old man stirred the fire with a branch. A shower of sparks rose and settled. Even on this mellow October night he could feel that old familiar chill creeping down his spine. It was a feeling he got whenever he recalled that night long ago when he had encountered the ghostly Chasse-Galerie.

"Well, boys, this was way back when I was about twelve and my brother, Jimbo, must have been fourteen. Papa told us not to go huntin', it bein' Sunday and all. But we wouldn't listen, *mais non.* We were both old enough to know better, of course, but we were full of ourselves.

"All day long we were just itchin' to run our dogs and get us some game. Mama and Papa had gone to visit her cousin. We didn't expect them back till way after dark, as they had to drive the wagon all the way to town and back. So, we boys snuck out in the early evenin' and turned Buster and Napoleon loose.

"Those dogs started cuttin' up all at once. They were hot on the trail of somethin' and we meant to get it. We were so busy followin' the hounds, we didn't realize how far we had gone from the house. I mean, we were way out back in the river bottoms.

"It was gettin' dark fast, when all of a sudden those dogs went crazy. They were yelpin' and howlin' like somebody was beatin' them. Jimbo and me, we took off runnin' towards all that ruckus. Pretty soon, here come those dogs, just beatin' a path outta there. We tried callin' the dogs back, but I swear they went wild. Somethin' had just about scared Buster and Napoleon to death.

"Next thing we knew, a big gush of wind was blowin', strong as any hurricane. The strangest sounds were comin' straight at us. Suddenly, we were surrounded by dogs barkin' and howlin'. There was no doubt in my mind but they were huntin' dogs. There were ringin' bells and rattlin' chains. Horns started to blow, 'Hooo, Hooo, Hooo.' There were voices of men hollerin', boomin' out like they were standin' right there beside us. We could hear those dogs racin' by and the footsteps of the men runnin' right through us. Only thing was, *nobody was there at all!*

"Well, those dogs beat us back to the house by only a hair. Papa was home by then, but he didn't punish us for goin' against him. He figured we had got the tar scared out of us for true.

"Buster and Napoleon never were the same again. They couldn't stand to hunt no more. Papa told us the Chasse-Galerie was those hunters who were cursed because they went huntin' on the Lord's Day. He told us boys that those haunted hunters and their ghost dogs visited each country every seven years. That's my story. That's just the way it happened. Me, I'm no liar. It's all true."

Shorty's eyes were big and round as he listened to the tale. Junior, however, looked at Pop as though the old man was crazy. "Now, Pop," he said, trying to keep a straight face, "that was a good story. Only thing is, you just about scared Shorty TO DEATH!" he hollered as he poked Shorty in the ribs.

Shorty was startled and nearly jumped out of his skin. "Aw, cut it out, Junior," he snapped, "I wasn't scared ..."

"Shhh," Pop said urgently, "Listen!"

A hush fell over the three men. Off in the distance they heard one of the dogs howling eerily in the night. "Hey, that's my dog," Junior said, standing up. "That's Bullet. Why, those other dogs aren't even close. There isn't a dog around that can keep up with Bullet. He's the fastest dog in three parishes, I guarantee. He's got somethin' good out there, *mais sho'*."

Junior grabbed his flashlight and gun. He was hurrying off when Pop spoke up, "Junior, where do you think you're goin?"

"Well, I'm goin' after that game, what else?" he exclaimed.

Pop eyed the younger man with concern. "Do you not realize," he asked, "that it is nearly midnight? Call your dog, Junior. You best not be hunting on Sunday."

Junior laughed and hitched up his pants. "Now, there is nothin' in this world that is gonna stop me from huntin', Sunday or not. I'm not church goin' like you, Pop. That ol' curse don't mean nothin' to me. Bullet has got somethin' cornered and he's yellin' his head off to get me to come get it. You boys just worry over ghosts all you want, but me, I'm goin' huntin'!" Junior disappeared into the darkness.

Pop checked his watch and shook his head. It was five minutes till midnight.

Junior hurried through the swamp woods, softly calling Bullet. At last he spotted the dog jumping under a tree, howling at a shadowy figure clinging to a high skinny limb. He shone his light up in the tree and saw two eyes gleaming down in the darkness. Why, it was the biggest, fattest raccoon he had seen in his whole life. Just wait till Pop got a look at this game!

Junior raised his .22 and took aim at the animal. It was a good clean shot. He was just about to squeeze the trigger when suddenly he heard the echoes of howling dogs approaching through the swamp woods. "Too late, Pop, this one is mine," he shouted. "Ya'll best stay back till I get her down."

He raised the gun again and WHAM! Suddenly, from out of nowhere, a mighty gust of wind knocked him off balance. "What the ... ?" He shone his light at the darkness. The beam only revealed the trees swaying to and fro as though they had come to life. "Pop? Shorty? Ya'll there?" he hollered. The wind threw his words back at him.

Just then he heard the sounds of a hunting party coming up on him at a fast clip. Howling dogs were running at him as wailing voices urged them on. Bells were ringing in his head and whistles pierced his brain. Chains rattled and clanked in his ears. Junior's flesh crawled and his heart pounded like a drum as the haunted hunters of the ghostly Chasse-Galerie flew over him, around him, through him.

Choking on fear, Junior turned around in circles firing his .22 at the thin air.

All at once the gun was wrenched from his hands. It flew up and came crashing down on his own head. At this Junior remembered his feet and burned the rubber off his tenny shoes getting out of those woods. He was streaking through the trees, his belly bouncing in time with the rhythm of his feet, when he overtook his dog. "Run, Bullet, run," he shouted. "Lead or follow, but *get out of my way!*"

Bullet was in just as much of a hurry to escape the Chasse-Galerie as his master. Scared as he was, that dog was not about to give Junior any ground. So together the two of them ran, tumbling over each other and squeezing through the thicket in a hollering, howling heap of fat and fur.

Back at camp, the other dogs had come in on their own accord. They growled and barked at the commotion out in the woods. Pop and Shorty shone their lights into the shadows, waiting and watching to see just what was going to emerge from the darkness.

At last they heard something coming at them, running like crazy and screaming like a panther. Pop trained his light on the spot while Shorty picked up his gun and took aim. Branches thrashed about wildly as Junior crashed through the thicket running ninety miles an hour. He had taken the lead and was purely outrunning the fastest dog in three parishes.

"Don't shoot!" he screamed. "Run for your lives, it's the haunted hunters of the Chasse-Galerie!"

Junior fairly flew past Pop and Shorty. "But we didn't hear nothin'," Shorty called, " 'cept you and Bullet!"

"Hey, Junior," Pop yelled, "come back. Where you runnin' off to?"

Away off in the distance they heard Junior holler back, "It's Sunday mornin', and me, I'm goin' to church, *right now!*"

The Grunch

There are countless lovers' lane stories that have grown up across the country. Here is an original tale created from many stories that have circulated among teenagers since the 1950s. I gathered anecdotes of confrontations with the Grunch from New Orleans residents and from accounts collected and published by folklorists. Although these stories are often told as cautionary tales or for entertainment, some people claim they or a friend of a friend have actually seen this horrible, rock-whizzing creature.

Tony Benoit was the king of French High. Everybody knew it: the students, the teachers, and especially Tony himself. Back in those days, when the kids all called him T'Boy, he was the girls' heart throb and the envy of every boy.

Tight Levis, white T-shirt rolled up over his biceps, and wavy, black hair slicked back with Dixie pomade made him look like a cross between Brando and Elvis. At least that's what the girls wrote to each other on notes they secretly passed around when the teacher's back was turned.

When they should have been concentrating on World

Lit., the girls daydreamed over T'Boy's big brown eyes instead. Imagining the possibilities of love, they scribbled in their notebooks in big, looping letters *Mrs. Tony Benoit* over and over, dotting the *i*'s with little hearts.

T'Boy had a way with the girls, for true. No girl in her right mind had ever turned down a date with him. With a snap of his fingers, just like that, he could date any girl at French High. The girls agreed, there was no doubt about it, T'Boy put the *ooh* in cool.

The boys admired the spell he cast over the girls, but it was his car that they really envied. T'Boy worked summers on a barge and had saved enough money to buy his dream car: a customized, pinstriped, cherry red '57 Chevy souped up with a 409 engine, four-barrel carburetor, overhead cams, and a dual exhaust. There wasn't a car that could come close to beating him in the Saturday night drag races out on Belle Bayou road. Once he revved up the motor and popped the clutch, T'Boy burned rubber like the devil, and then he was outta there like a flash of lightnin'.

T'Boy loved his red, shiny baby more than anything. He called her Betty Lou and kept her washed and waxed until her chrome gleamed and her bright paint glowed. He pampered that Chevy and watched over her like a jealous boyfriend. He had all the girlfriends he wanted, but Betty Lou was his only true love. She was perfect in every way. Not a dent or a scratch dimmed her beauty, and her fine-tuned engine purred like a tiger.

If he ever met up with a girl that could match Betty Lou for looks, speed, and fire, why he'd give her his heart and his senior ring too. But the girls he knew were more interested in keeping their teased hairdos unruffled than they were in adventure. *Nope,* he thought, *there's not a girl that can hold a candle to Betty Lou.*

In his red Chevy T'Boy cruised New Orleans like he was royalty. Little did he know, his kingdom was about to be rocked by a five-foot-two, eyes-of-blue, ponytail-hangin'-down girl by the name of Irene. It was plain from the start, this new girl was going to be trouble.

He had ambled up to her wearing his best Elvis-like sneer and snapped his fingers. "You and me, Saturday night, the Burger Hut, be there."

Instead of giggling a bubbly yes like he expected, she made a face and said sourly, "I don't think so. I don't go out with gorillas, and you," she said with a snap of her fingers, "are a big, stuck-up ape!"

Pulling out his comb, he slid it through his high hair nonchalantly, as though he didn't care one bit that the girl had turned him down. But it was no use. Everybody had seen the king of French High disgraced. At lunch the girls were giggling and whispering among themselves. The boys punched him in the arm and said with a smirk, "Win some, lose some" and "Nice try, buddy."

"Hey, man," he said, "if I really wanted a date with her, I'd get it, no problem. That girl, what's her name? Irene? She's just playing hard to get!"

"Oh yeah," they all said, "then prove it. We dare you to get her to go to the homecoming dance with you."

"That's a stupid dare," T'Boy said with scorn. "I don't

even like the girl."

"UH-OH," the girls teased, "what's the matter, 'fraid you're gonna lose? Maybe you're not so cool after all."

T'Boy saw he was never going to live this down. A snip of a girl had made him a laughing stock. All right then, he'd show them all—especially Irene.

"OK then, here's the bet," he said with a swagger. "I betcha I can get that girl to go to the homecoming dance, *and*, afterwards, I'll even take her to Grunch Lane! After the dance, ya'll go out on Belle Bayou road. Ya'll can see my signal from there. I'll flash my headlights three times at midnight. That'll prove we're there. Got it?"

Everyone looked at him with renewed respect. Grunch Lane. Nobody went out there, not if they could help it. Occasionally the boys would race down the shadowy remote road on a dare, but it was dangerous to linger. Once, the dark gravel road was a favorite parking spot for young couples, but that was twenty years ago, before the Grunch came to live on the lane. Since then, the stories of his attacks on couples had grown with each graduating class.

According to witnesses who had managed to escape his wrath, the Grunch was a horrible sight. He was a four-legged, two-armed monster, half man and half sheep. His lower body and four legs were those of a sheep, but he had the chest, arms, and head of a man. He was covered all over with greasy, gray, woolly hair. His large, dark eyes were glassy, and the coiled, sharp horns of a ram crowned his head.

The Grunch tolerated no intruders on his lonely lane.

He surprised unsuspecting couples by leaping from the dense bushes onto their parked car. He would jump up and down on the hood, bleating a dreadful cry. Then, as the terrified driver tried to speed away, the Grunch would hurl rocks at the car. Many a dented hood and broken windshield had been offered up as evidence that the Grunch was real.

A few daredevils had tried to photograph the Grunch but the pictures always came out fuzzy and blurred. Of course, there were skeptics. They declared that the Grunch was just superstition, or teenagers playing practical jokes. Many had set out to prove the monster didn't exist, but once they'd been down on Grunch Lane they changed their minds. It was easy to believe that something strange lived on that lonesome road. Despite all the attempts to prove the creature was a hoax, the Grunch remained an unsolved mystery.

T'Boy knew he had to do something big, something really cool to turn the tables on Irene. Grunch Lane was his trump. Maybe all those other babies were scared of the Grunch, but not him. But how to trick the girl into going with him? *She must have moved here from the sticks,* he thought ruefully, *or she would have jumped at the chance to go out with me.*

Suddenly he had an idea. *OK, Miz Irene, you think you're so tough, then let's just see your stuff,* he thought. *Man, this is beautiful. All I gotta do is dare her. Yeah, she'll fall for it all right, and when she does ol' T'Boy's gonna arrange for her to get the scare of her life!*

The news of the bet spread like wildfire until it reached the ears of the new girl, Irene. *Well,* she thought, *Mr. Stuck-up Apeman has got some nerve. This is going to be one bet he is gonna lose.*

The next day T'Boy played his hand. "So, Irene," he said, "how's about you go to the dance with me, and if you're lucky, I'll take you out to Grunch Lane afterwards."

Irene looked at him with a bored expression and popped her bubblegum. "I wouldn't go with you if you were the last boy on the planet."

"Ooh," T'Boy smirked, "you really put me down. This is one tough girl," he told the crowd that was gathering around them. "Maybe you don't like me—or maybe you're just scared of the Grunch!"

Irene rolled her eyes. "Scared of some stupid story? I was raised in the swamp, and I know all about that kind of stuff. I'm not scared of the *fifolet,* or the *rougarou,* or ghosts, or any ol' Grunch!"

The crowd was beginning to snicker at T'Boy again. "OK," he said with a big grin, "I triple dare you to prove you're not scared of the Grunch. You go to the dance with me, and then we'll go out to the lane. No matter what happens, if you scream out on Grunch Road, then you gotta wash my car our whole senior year."

Irene narrowed her eyes and considered the dare. *He's up to something,* she thought, *but maybe I can beat him at his own game.* "Yeah, but if you holler first," she said, calling his bluff, "then I get to drive your car every Saturday night until graduation!" She stood back, hands on her hips, smiling like the cat that ate the canary.

T'Boy hesitated for a moment. That girl, driving his Betty Lou? Never. But there was no way he was gonna lose, not with an ace up his sleeve. "OK," he said, "it's a bet." T'Boy and Irene shook hands on the deal.

The homecoming dance was two weeks away. Irene and T'Boy passed each other in the hall, giving each other the cold shoulder. Everybody was gossiping about the whole thing and making predictions about the outcome.

Some of the girls tried to discourage Irene from going to Grunch Lane. They told her the dark tales of the attacks, and of a couple that ran out of gas on the lane. They just disappeared. Nobody ever found them, but their car was all beat-up and dented. "There were tracks too," they whispered with big eyes, "sheep tracks."

Irene wasn't bothered by their warning. "I grew up listenin' to my *grandmaman* tellin' me about swamp creatures and bayou bogeymen," she said. "Even if I believed in that kind of thing, I wouldn't be scared. My *grandmaman* taught me all the ol' Cajun ways for scarin' away evil. So," she said with a smile, "you don't have to worry about me. Besides, it's high time some girl stood up to T'Boy. Who does he think he is anyway, snapping his fingers like that at us?"

The girls had never thought of this before. Yeah, they agreed, who does he think he is? It wasn't long before "The Bet," as it came to be known, divided the 1963 senior class: girls for Irene and boys for T'Boy.

At last homecoming night arrived. T'Boy drove Irene

to the dance in Betty Lou. He had to admit she looked great in her blue dress and corsage. Irene hugged the car door and stole glances at T'Boy, thinking he was handsome even if he was a conceited ape. At the dance T'Boy joined the boys, and Irene stood laughing with the girls.

At 11:30 exactly, everyone jumped in their cars. The crowd headed for Belle Bayou Road while T'Boy and Irene drove toward Grunch Lane. T'Boy checked his watch. Everything was perfect. What a scheme he'd cooked up. Irene was going to get the daylights scared out of her. All he needed was a spooky setting like Grunch Lane and a little clever assistance. It hadn't been difficult to find a chump willing to do his dirty work. Everybody wanted to get in good with the king. He needed a guy who could keep his mouth shut. Who else but Benjamin Oliver, otherwise known as B.O., the class nerd?

It was B.O. who had worked out the costume, a concoction of dyed cotton balls, papier-mâché, wire, and face paint. He had to hand it to the guy, it was a great outfit. B.O. would be at Grunch lane already, his car hidden in a grove of bushes. With Irene's imagination primed and the dark lonely lane looming before them, B.O. would really look like the Grunch when he jumped out of the thicket.

T'Boy planned it down to the second. At exactly twelve midnight he'd flash his headlights three times. The crowd over at Belle Bayou road would see the signal and know the couple was at Grunch Lane. He'd casually roll his window down. At 12:01 B.O. would jump out in his Grunch get-up, bleating and jumping around like crazy. The eager group waiting just ahead would be sure to hear Irene's screams echoing through the night.

Once T'Boy was satisfied everybody had heard Irene scream, they'd all meet back at the Belle Bayou Bridge. B.O. would lay low till they were gone and then sneak unseen from the lane. Everybody would think T'Boy was a hero. Irene was gonna eat crow. Nobody would be wise to the trick, except for B.O., and he knew he better keep his trap shut, or else.

The lights of the city faded behind T'Boy and Irene as they drove along the gravel road that led to the lane. Thick bushes hovered on either side of the narrow, twisting path. A harvest moon hung in the sky, and gusts of wind rattled through the leaves. They drove slowly into Grunch Lane and parked at the designated place, a gloomy spot beside a great live oak tree.

They sat in silence for awhile, listening to the night sounds around them. T'Boy glanced at the time. It was thirty seconds to midnight. He flashed his headlights three times. Up ahead, three flashes returned his signal.

All right, he thought gleefully, *The Grunch is gonna appear anytime now.* He rolled his window down. Irene didn't seem to notice; she was too busy fidgeting with her camera. "You brought a camera?" he asked with a laugh. "I thought you didn't believe in the Grunch."

"Well, if anything weird does happen," she said with mock sweetness, "I want to get a picture of you yellin' your head off."

T'Boy was getting impatient. It was a quarter past

138

midnight. Where was B.O.? The minutes ticked by slowly. "Well," Irene said with a yawn, "it doesn't look like the Grunch is gonna show his ol' ugly self tonight. We might as well get goin'. It's gettin' late."

T'Boy turned to Irene. "Aw, come on, just a little longer. Let's wait just five more min—" Suddenly he stopped speaking. Irene was looking at him, her eyes wide with fear. In the moonlight she looked pale as a ghost. "What?" he said, "Quit tryin' to pull my leg, there's nothin' behind me but ..." T'Boy nearly jumped out of his skin when he turned and looked out.

Standing less than a yard from the car was the Grunch. *Wow,* he thought excitedly, *what a costume! That B.O. is a genius. Those ram's horns are great! How in the world did he get his eyes to look so black and shiny?* Irene still hadn't screamed, but she was white as a sheet and shaking so hard she could barely keep her camera in her hands. Just then, the phony Grunch jumped on Betty Lou's hood. Up and down he pounded, rocking the car and denting the metal with his hooves. His shrill bleating filled the air.

"Hey, my car," T'Boy exclaimed angrily, "that jerk is denting my car!" This seemed only to enrage the fake Grunch further. He threw his monstrous body down heavily on the Chevy's hood. Then, pressing his horrid gray woolly face against the driver's side of the windshield glass, he let loose a blood curdling shriek. T'Boy's eyes bugged out and his jaw dropped. Had B.O. gone mad?

Suddenly the flash bulb exploded. The Grunch screamed with pain and rolled off the hood. For a moment he staggered away, blinded by the light, only to circle around to Irene's door. With terrific force he pulled the door open and snatched the horrified girl's camera. He raised it high in his hairy hands, snorting and stomping his hooves in triumph.

Now Irene found her voice. "Wait just a minute you big, ugly bag o' wool, that's my camera!" To T'Boy's astonishment, she jumped out of the car and grabbed the camera. He couldn't believe his luck. She was supposed to be screaming bloody murder by now, and instead she was playing tug of war with the Grunch!

At last Irene fell backwards, still holding the camera. She ran for the car and jumped in, locking the door behind her. The creature bleated with rage and suddenly disappeared.

"Come on," urged Irene, "here's our chance. Let's get out of here!"

T'Boy was fed up with his practical joke. That stupid nerd had dented Betty Lou. B.O. was gonna pay for that! T'Boy turned on his headlights and saw, to his dismay, the Grunch running towards the Chevy clutching an armful of rocks.

The bogus bogeyman began hurling rocks at the Chevy. Boom! A huge scrape on the door. Crack! There went the windshield. Bang! A rock dented the fender. "That's it!" T'Boy warned through clenched teeth, "he's gone too far! A joke is a joke, but this isn't funny." He switched on the motor and revved up the engine. "You creep, look at my car! B.O., you better run for your life!"

He popped the clutch and the car screeched into action.

T'Boy suddenly realized he'd let the cat out of the bag. "Now, Irene," he began, "I can explain ..."

"Well," she hissed, "of all the stupid, low-down, rotten, mean jokes to play! T'Boy you *are* a gorilla. You make B.O. in that Grunch get-up look like Einstein! He almost wrecked my camera. I'm glad he busted your car up. You deserve a lot worse!"

They argued all the way down the lane. When they pulled up and parked on Belle Bayou Road they were still fighting. The crowd gathered around them asking questions." What happened? Who was doing all that awful screeching? Did you see him, did you see the Grunch?"

"Shh, pipe down, somebody's coming."

Sure enough, a pair of headlights was approaching. A big station wagon pulled up beside the group and stopped. The door opened and a sheepish B.O. stepped out.

Before he could say a word, T'Boy jumped on him and they fell in the dirt. "Look what you did to my car, you little twirp. You're gonna get it now!"

"Hey, I didn't do nothin'," B.O. yelled. "That's what I came out here to tell you. I couldn't get the car till late. My dad had a bowling tournament. I'm tellin' the truth. I didn't do nothin' to your car, I just got here!"

Something really strange was going on. There was no way B.O. could have got out of his costume and driven up there so quickly. And those eyes and horns—could B.O. really have faked them?

T'Boy felt a chill run down his spine. He looked at

Irene. She stared wide-eyed down at her camera and up at him. "But, if it w-wasn't B.O.," she stammered, "w-what was that horrible thing b-back there?" All bets were off when T'Boy and Irene suddenly screamed loud enough to wake the dead, "It really was ... THE GRUNCH!"

Betty Lou never was the same after that, and neither was T'Boy. He didn't mind the scratches and dents on his Chevy now that he had found his dream girl. Irene had it all: beauty, brains—and any girl who would wrestle the Grunch had to have guts. Irene framed the snapshot and hung it over the mantel beside the pictures of their wedding.

Years later, when their kids asked how they met, Tony and Irene told them the story of how the Grunch brought them together. They showed them the amazing photograph. "Wow!" the kids exclaimed, "that Grunch is really ugly! Look at his big ol' eyes and his wide open jaws ..."

"No, children," Irene corrected, pointing to a fuzzy pale blur in the snapshot. "*There's* the Grunch. That *other* bug-eyed, slack-jawed monster is your daddy!"

The Werewolf Bridegroom

The Cajun werewolf, known as the loupgarou *or* rougarou, *prowled the swamps and bayous of Louisiana long before science sent him howling into legend. But the stories survive into this century. To this day, rare sightings of the* loupgarou *are still reported. There are yet people who believe in the curse of the werewolf. The best protection against the* rougarou *is to lay thirteen small objects, such as beans, at the door. The creature is forced to count them all before entering. Since the* loupgarou *cannot count higher than twelve, he must count the objects over and over until the burning light of the rising sun frightens him away.*

Dupré studied the smooth face of the young man before him. His eyes had grown dim with age, but he could tell his great-grandson thought he was an old fool. It was true his mind wandered these days. It puzzled him that he often couldn't remember what he'd done the day before, but he could recall the events of sixty-five years ago as though they had only just happened. *Mon Dieu,* he thought, *has it been so long since I was Willy's age?*

Suddenly the old man's thin frame was wracked by a gut wrenching fit of coughing. He hacked until his ribs ached and his face purpled. At last Dupré caught a ragged

breath. The young man was looking at him with alarm. "You want I should get you some water?" he asked.

"What I want," said Dupré, catching his breath, "is to talk to you. There is gossip around town. They say you have sworn to kill Leo Guidry if he marries that red-headed girl you used to go around with."

The young man shifted uneasily in his chair. He looked down from the *galerie* at the bayou snaking lazily before them. "I don't know what you're talkin' about, Grandpapa," he said with a sideways glance at the old man. "Maybe you shouldn't listen to gossip."

"I only listen when I know it's true. Willy, why you want to kill this man?" asked Dupré. "That woman don't want you. She is gonna marry Leo this very Sunday."

The young man's face darkened with anger. "Rose loves me, I know it. It's that Leo, it's all his doin'. He's got her all confused. But he can't have her. She belongs to me. I'll find a way to stop that wedding," Willy said through clenched teeth, "even if I have to ..."

"Sell your soul to the devil?" the old man broke in. "You think that is just talk too? I am old, and I have seen much in my time." He lowered his voice. "I tell you the evil one is real."

"Grandpapa, your head is filled with all that old-time superstition," Willy said with disgust. "Maybe you believe it, but I don't. Stay out of this, I know what I'm doing." The young man's eyes narrowed. "I'll get rid of him. There are ways. Nobody will ever know."

Dupré shook his head. "Ah, now I see, then Rose will

want you?" Suddenly the old man spat. "Are you blind, Willy? Rose does not love you. She will never stop lovin' Leo. The truth is in her eyes. It is a look I have seen before."

"What are you talking about?" Willy said angrily. "You don't know anything about Rose—or me!"

"I know all I need to know," said Dupré. "Even now the evil one tempts you. He has returned from the shadows to tease me. I defeated his servant once, and now he has come again. He thinks he will punish me if he destroys my own flesh and blood. You are the one he's been waitin' for all this time. Your dark wishes and your thirst for revenge have called him back to this world. I can still fight him, Willy, but I can't do it alone."

The young man looked at his great-grandfather and felt the flesh creep on the back of his neck. The old man's eyes burned with a strange fire as he laid his hand on Willy's shoulder. "Listen to my story. It is a secret I have kept for sixty-five years. All along I knew that evil one would come back. I have watched for him all this long time. He will not win your soul, not while there is breath in my body to fight him."

Dupré rocked slowly in his creaking chair. Around him a steady breeze had begun to blow. Heat lightning danced in the half-dark sky. Off in the distance thunder rumbled like a rattler sounding its warning. As the old man began to speak, time stopped for the space of a heartbeat and flowed backwards.

"I was twenty, about your age, when I first laid eyes on her. She was the most beautiful girl I ever saw. Her long hair was chestnut-colored. It shined like copper in the sun. Her eyes were as green as the swamp. There was something between us from that moment on. We didn't speak of it in the beginning. It wasn't proper. But in time, everybody knew, Dupré and Katrin loved one another.

"She lived with her family, poor people, like most of us Cajuns were back then. Her papa gave me permission to court his girl. We were seein' each other regular, courtin' like all the young people did in them days. Every Saturday night somebody had the *fais-dodo* dance at their *cabane.* Katrin and me, we danced all night and went to Mass the next mornin'. It wasn't long before I asked for her hand in marriage. We were to be married in one month. Ah, those were happy times. All I hoped and prayed for was coming true.

"But one night at a dance some fellas come up and warned me not to see Katrin anymore. Said she belonged to another, the son of the richest man in the parish. If I knew what was good for me, I'd leave that girl alone. Katrin swore she would love me forever but I was afraid of losing her to this wealthy man.

"The next Saturday he showed up at the dance. Like you, his name was William, but of course we didn't speak the English in those days. We called him by his French name, Guillaume. As soon as I saw him, I knew he was evil through and through. There was somethin' mean and hard in his eyes. When he looked at Katrin, I felt my blood run cold. We both loved that girl with hearts that burned like fire. I was willing to die for my Katrin, but Guillaume was willing to kill.

"When I tell you what happened, you will think I have gone mad. But what I'm gonna tell you is true. I will swear it on the grave of my *chère* Katrin. May she look down on you, her great-grandson, and help you through your trouble.

"One black night I was walkin' on the bayou road, coming home from visitin' Katrin. Guillaume sneaked up on me and grabbed me from behind. He held a knife to my throat. His hot breath smelled of bad whiskey, but there was something else too: he reeked of pure hatred.

"'Now it is just you and me,' he whispered in my ear. 'There is nobody to see if I slit your throat. I could throw your body in the bayou or bury you in the swamp woods, but Katrin would only wait for you to return. *Mais non*, there is a better way to get rid of you,' he said with a wicked laugh. 'I will destroy you and put an end to Katrin's love. When I am done, she will feel only horror for you. She will never marry you. Katrin will be my bride! You are cursed, Dupré. It is time for you to taste your defeat!'

"Suddenly his sharp blade pricked my neck. Blood trickled down my collar. Then Guillaume spoke strange words over me. I struggled against him, but a great weariness came over me and I slumped to the ground. The last thing I remember before I passed out was the sound of Guillaume's wild laughter. But it was not the voice of a man that I heard. It was the evil one who mocked me.

"When I waked the sun was shinin'. I thought I must have been dreamin' until I saw the dried blood on my hands. *Next time*, I thought, *I will be ready for him.* I would never give up Katrin to him, never!

"I walked back to my *cabane* slowly. I had bled a little, but otherwise I was all right. Yet I trembled like a leaf. Each day was worse than the one before. On the third day I discovered the cause. In my coat pocket I found a charm. It was spotted with my blood. So that was it. Guillaume had made a *gris-gris* on me.

"I knew where he got the charm. There was an ol' woman who lived way back in the swamp who told fortunes and made potions. It was said she had mastered the dark powers. Her *gris-gris* charms were nothin' more than ol' women's talk to me. But why was I gettin' weaker everyday? I was afraid to tell anyone, especially Katrin. I knew no doctor could help me, no *traiteur* could cure me.

"For a month I hid my sickness and my fear. Each night I lay in bed, burnin' up with fever, tortured by nightmares. What was happenin' to me? What spell had the *gris-gris* woman sold to Guillaume? At last I learned the terrible truth. It was the night of the full moon. I was so sick with the fever I thought I would surely die. But I soon found out that Guillaume had cursed me with a fate worse than death.

"Before my own eyes, my body began to twist and coil like a snake. My arms and legs changed into those of a beast. My hands and feet sprouted sharp nails. Hair grew on my body until I was covered with a shaggy hide. I rushed to the mirror, and I saw the horrible thing

Guillaume had done to me. He had laid the curse of the werewolf on me. I was doomed to roam every night as a *loupgarou!*

"I cried out, but my voice rose like the howlin' of the wolf. Until dawn I was trapped in this creature's body. Now I understood Guillaume's threats. Katrin could never love me this way. All my dreams were lost. I leaped into the moonlight with murder in my heart. I meant to find Guillaume and kill him.

"All night I prowled along the bayou, but my enemy was nowhere to be found. Dogs barked and chased me through the woods. I dared not be caught, for I was certain to be mistaken for a mad dog or a wolf. The people of the village, my friends and relatives, would kill me on the spot. Death would be a welcome end to this horror, but I could not leave Katrin alone to fall into Guillaume's evil hands.

"I hid myself in the swamp the rest of the night. At last I fell into a deep sleep. When I waked, it was morning. I was filthy and scratched all over, but I rejoiced—I was a man again. I knew I could never go back to the village as a *loupgarou* man. I had to find a way to break the curse. Katrin would be heartbroken at my disappearance, but I could not tell her the truth. My only hope was to go to the *gris-gris* woman.

"For two days I wandered through the swamp. Each night the horror came over me, and I changed back into a *loupgarou.* In that shape I hunted like an animal. In the dawn when I waked, my hunger was satisfied. My clothes were torn and blood-stained. It sickened me to think what prey I had caught and eaten in the night.

"On the third day, I found the ol' woman's *cabane*. She sat huddled in her shawl like a spider waitin' in its web. Her mossy hair was tangled, and her bony arms were knotted like the *boscoyo*. Warts grew on her gray face. 'Ah, Dupré, I've been expecting you,' she said. 'So, now you have found me. What is it you want?'

"'You gotta help me,' I begged. 'Free me from the curse of the *rougarou*. Break the *gris-gris*, lift the spell!'

"The toothless hag cackled at me. 'Dupré, you are a poor man. How will you pay?' she asked.

"'I have no money—but I will get it. Free me and I will bring you the money. I swear it.'

"She howled with laughter at my words. 'You are as stupid as the other one who came before you. "Make me a *gris-gris*," he whines, "I have money. I am rich, I can pay." I told him, just like I'll tell you. It's not money that my master wants. What use has he for money? He wants more, much more. He is the master, I am only his tool. I can make a *gris-gris* to free you, but he is the one you must pay. His price is—your soul! Guillaume paid dearly to curse you. To satisfy his hatred, he sold his soul to my master. Now he is forever doomed.'

"Suddenly the *gris-gris* woman hissed at me, 'Be quick, *vite!* What is your answer? Will you pay for your freedom?'

"Temptation swept over me like a hurricane. I imagined Guillaume holding Katrin in his greedy arms. Then it was as if I heard my *chère* whisperin' to me.

'Forever,' she said, 'I will love you forever.' All at once I saw the trap. I might have Katrin in this life, but I would spend eternity without her. I could think of no greater torture. 'No, I will not pay your master! There must be a way to break the spell. My love for Katrin is stronger than Guillaume's hatred. *Le Bon Dieu* will help me ...'

"The hag doubled over and let out a dreadful moan, 'Do not speak that name to me, it burns me like fire!'

"Through my fear and fever I saw her weakness. I spoke again, this time louder, 'Yes, *Le Bon Dieu* will hear my prayer ...'

" 'Stop it,' she whined. 'Do not say His name!'

" 'Woman, I will say it again and again until you are scorched,' I hollered. 'Tell me how to break the spell!'

" 'I will tell you,' she screeched, 'but do not think you will escape my master's wrath so easily. He'll get his revenge yet! To break the spell,' she said, 'is to risk death. You must provoke a human into drawing your blood. That done, you will become a man again. Tell the human your name. If he reveals your secret before a year is gone by, then your savior will take on the curse. He will become a *loupgarou!* But,' she cackled, 'the human will most likely kill you anyway. That will make my master very happy.'

"I ran from that gruesome woman as fast as I could. My heart was pounding with hope. The spell could be broken! She was right, I would risk death to free myself from the curse, but it was a chance I would gladly take. I couldn't live my life half man and half beast. To live without the love of Katrin was worse than death to me.

"It was almost dark, and I could feel the fever comin' on me. Soon I changed into a panting *loupgarou*. Now, to find a human to help me break the *gris-gris*. I prowled along the bayou road, waiting for someone to come along. Suddenly I heard the step of a man walking ahead of me in the distance. I followed him silently for awhile. When I was close, I lunged forward at the man's heels. My growlin' and snappin' startled him. With my animal senses I could smell his fear. He whirled around holdin' a small sharp knife. In the darkness he fell upon me. His blade stabbed my right paw again and again. I fell to the ground crippled and bloody.

"All of a sudden my body began to twist and coil as I changed back into a man. I was free of the spell! But when I looked into the man's horrified face, my joy was boundless. 'So, it is you,' I said, 'the one who cursed me has now set me free! Guillaume, aren't you happy to see your old friend Dupré? You have lost, Guillaume. There is nothing you can do—Katrin is mine and we will be married. This time the trap has caught the hunter. You dare not tell Katrin that her bridegroom was a *loupgarou*. If you reveal the secret before a year has passed, then you will inherit the very *gris-gris* you made on me. You will become a *loupgarou!* You had your chance to kill me,' I said, 'but fear made you miss your mark. Now that I know you and the one you serve, I'll never turn my back to you again. I pity you, Guillaume. You sold your soul to the evil one, and all for nothin'. You did not win Katrin and you did not defeat me!'

" 'It's not over yet,' he warned. 'I'll come back, in this life and the next. I will have my revenge. If you should escape me by death, then I'll wait for the generations that follow you and Katrin. One of them will be weak, Dupré, and that's the one who will pay with his soul. My master demands it, and I will obey. Now, mon padnat,' he snarled, 'let us play our hands to the finish, eh?'

"With those words, Guillaume leaped into the dark night and disappeared.

"I waited three days before returning to the village. I could not go to Katrin as I was, ragged and bleeding. But when I came to her, I found she knew my secret. Guillaume had already told her the truth: the man she loved, the man she would marry, had been a *loupgarou*. She came to me and took my right hand. There in my palm were three fresh wounds. She kissed my hand. I will never forget the look of love in her eyes.

" 'I lost you once, *cher*,' she whispered, 'but never again. Whatever you were doesn't matter. Nothing can keep us apart. What happened will be our secret.'

"In one month we were to be married. Everyone was buzzin' with the news. A *fais-dodo* was gonna be held that Saturday night after the wedding. When at last we made our vows to each other I thought we were safe. But I had forgotten Guillaume's threats.

"The *fais-dodo* started up. Everybody was singin' and dancin' to the fiddlin'. A great bonfire was burned in celebration of our marriage. Katrin was waltzin' in my arms, when suddenly, we heard screams. *"Loupgarou,*

loupgarou!" they cried. I turned to see a great shaggy beast standing in the ring of firelight. His sides heaved, and foam flecked his bared fangs. His eyes burned with hate. I spoke not a word, but I knew that Guillaume was the *loupgarou* who stood before me.

"I pushed Katrin away as the creature jumped for my throat. We fell to the ground struggling. Over and over we rolled, closer to the fire. I could see my own reflection in the beast's eyes. I was growing weaker, and blood dripped from the wounds in my hand. All at once Katrin screamed my name and threw somethin' on the ground near me. I held the werewolf with my left hand as my right hand searched and found a cold, sharp butcher knife. With all my strength, I plunged the knife into the beast.

"The *loupgarou* howled with pain and leaped back into the black night. A search was made, but the beast had disappeared into thin air. Only I knew where to find it. The next morning at dawn, I slipped out unseen and made my way toward the *cabane* of the *gris-gris* woman. At last I found a fresh trail of blood and followed it. In the first light of the risin' sun I found him. He was layin' on his back so quiet I thought he was dead. But then, to my horror, I saw—the knife.

"It was stuck handle-deep in his chest. With each beat of his dyin' heart, the knife jerked in rhythm. For a moment, his eyes opened wide. He was trying to speak to me. I leaned down and he hissed, 'I'll ... be ... back!' His heart beat slower and slower until the knife blade shuddered in his chest and was still. I felt only pity when I looked at the dead body of Guillaume, the man. The knife had freed him from the curse of the werewolf, but he still owed his soul to the devil for all of eternity.

"I buried him in secret. Nobody ever discovered what became of the rich man's son Guillaume. Katrin never told a soul. Me, I have kept silent until now. To this day I still carry the mark of the *loupgarou* in my palm."

The old man suddenly fell silent and looked around him. The wind was whipping through the trees and pushing angry black clouds through the sky. "Looks like we got some weather headed this way. We best go in," he said, turning to his great-grandson.

Something about the young man's face stopped him cold. "Willy," he said, "what is it? What's wrong with you?"

Willy began to laugh. Dupré felt his heart pound with a hard, sickening thud. "So, it has come to this," he said.

"Come to what, you ol' fool?" the young man hissed. "All your talkin' won't stop me from getting what I want. I mean to have my revenge."

"It has been sixty-five years," Dupré said calmly, "but I have not forgotten the sound of your laughter. I'd know you anywhere, Guillaume. Where is Willy, what have you done with the boy?"

"He is here with me, of course. After all, he is the one who summoned me. He has promised my master his soul in exchange for a *gris-gris*. He wants a curse to destroy a man. And I," laughed the voice, "am going to give him what he wants!"

"He will not listen to you," Dupré warned. "Now he knows what you are and who you serve. You are too late, Guillaume. I have told him the truth. You did not win before; you won't win now."

Suddenly the wind rose to a wail. A blinding bolt of lightning lit up the purple sky. Its thunderclap shook the earth. "Do you think you will stop me with a story?" the voice laughed scornfully. "Look at you, Dupré, you have one foot in the grave already. You cling to life by a thread. Even now you gasp for breath. The years have made you weak but I have grown stronger. Old man, you don't have the strength to resist me!"

"I wasn't talkin' about me. It is Willy who has got to fight you, he's the one with the power to boot you back to hell. All this time I have watched and waited for you to return, thinking I could stop you. But now I know it's not up to me anymore. Your master is powerful, Guillaume. He can bend the trees with wind and cut the sky with lightnin', but can he sway the heart of a good man?"

"No!" spat Dupré. "Willy is a good man, I'd stake my soul on it! So now, let us, as you once said, play our hand to the finish, eh? My Willie against your bluff."

Dupré sat back in his chair and rocked, watching his great-grandson like a cat. All around him, the wind howled with fury. Blue lightning flashed on the old man's white hair. He drew a ragged breath and raised his voice to the young man before him.

"Listen to me, Willy," he shouted over the raging

storm. "Shut him out, don't let him into your heart! He has found you by the weakness you hold inside. He will destroy you by your hatred, just as he himself was destroyed. Do not sell your soul and think you can buy love; murder will cost you eternity. Forever is too high a price to pay. If you must kill, then kill your own hatred. If you must destroy, then destroy the spirit of evil within your heart and live in peace."

The storm unleashed all its fury now as heaven and hell struggled to win the soul of one man. Lightning hit a live oak and split the ancient tree into a burning fork. Suddenly Willy shook his head like a dreamer waking from a nightmare. He raised his hands to the heavens and screamed into the wind, "Noooo!" It was the last thing the old man knew before he was knocked out of his shoes by a lightning bolt.

Dupré could hear someone calling his name in the darkness that swirled around him. "Willy, he whispered, is that you? I can't see you. Well, it don't matter. Willy," he said to the hand that held his own, "you done good, son. You whupped 'im good. I knew you could do it! I'm proud of you. It's up to you now, boy, you keep the truth, and watch out for them that's comin'—the children of your children and all our flesh and blood that follow. Willy? You wait and watch, 'cause that one, he'll be back. His master will always send him back lookin' for troubled souls."

"Hush now," a voice said softly. "Willy, can't hear you no more. You're with me, *cher.*"

The darkness was burning away from his eyes like morning fog on the bayou. A fine mist of colors collected like dew in his sight: swamp green, golden sun and shining copper. Then the colors blossomed into the face of his beloved. It was just like the first time he saw her sixty-five years ago. Her loving green eyes gazed down at him, and her chestnut hair glinted in the sunlight like a new copper penny.

"Katrin," he said in wonder, "it's you. I missed you so much—it's been so long." He reached his fingertips to her hair and was amazed to see his arm, strong and young again. Slowly Dupré turned his right hand over and looked at his palm. The mark of the *loupgarou* was gone.

"*Chère*," he asked, "where are we? What is this place?"

Katrin smiled. "Forever, Dupré. This is forever."

Dupré laughed and drew a long, deep breath of sweet peace.

Glossary

- *beaucoup* a lot of something

- *bébé* baby

- *belle* beautiful

- *belle-mère* step-mother

- *bonsoir* good evening, good night

- *bon matin,* good morning

- *boscoyo* cypress knees, the protruding roots of the cypress tree

- *ça va?* how's it going?

- *café au lait* coffee with milk

- *café noir* black coffee

- *cabane* cabin, shack

- *chasse-galerie* ghostly hunting party

- *cauchemar* a nightmare witch said to ride its victims while they sleep; a nightmare

- *cemetière* cemetery

- *cher (m.); chère (f.)* dear

- *cheri* dear one; cherished

- *chicot* stump

- *chaud* hot

- *chouette* owl

- *comment ça va?* how's it going?

- *congo* poisonous water moccasin, also called cottonmouth

- *demi-tasse* a fancy, small porcelain or china cup

- *des z'onions* in standard french *des onions*, some onions

- *donne-moi des z'onions* give me some onions

- *fais-dodo* all-night dance

- *fifolet* a floating ball of light seen in the swamp; will 'o the wisp; phosphorescent swamp gas

- *galerie* front porch

- *garde-soleil* sun bonnet

- *goujon* mud catfish; yellow catfish

- *grands doights* long fingers

- *grand (m.); grande (f.)* great or big

- *grand beaucoup* a great amount of something

- *grandmaman* grandmother

- *grand-père* grandfather

- *gris-gris* magic charm; spell

- *joie de vivre* joy of living

- *jolie fille* pretty girl

- *le Bon Dieu*   the Good Lord

- *loup-garou*   werewolf

- *mon (m.); ma (f.)*   my

- *ma p'tite chère*   my little dear one

- *Madam; Madame*   Mrs. or Ma'am

- *mais non*   but no; of course not

- *mais oui*   but yes; of course

- *mais sho'*   sure; but of course

- *malheur*   misfortune; hard times

- *maman*   mama

- *maringoin*   mosquito

- *merci beaucoup*   thank you very much

- *mon padnat*   my partner, my buddy

- *M'sieur; Monsieur*   Mr.

- *non*   no

- *padnat*   buddy, friend

- *pauvre*   poor

- *pirogue*   a flat-bottom skiff or boat sometimes crafted in the manner of a dugout canoe

- *pourquoi*   why; type of folktale which explains how or why something came to be

- *p'tite*   little; little one

- *rougarou*   slang for loup-garou or werewolf

- *tante*   aunt

- *'tee fer*   little iron; iron triangle struck with iron rod to keep rhythm in traditional Cajun music

- *'tite*   little, small

- *traiteur*   healer

- *très*   very

- *très chaud*   very hot

- *viens avec moi*   come with me

- *vite*   quick, fast

- *wawaron*   bullfrog

- *z'onion*   a common pronunciation of *onion* or *onions*